THE
TEMPLE
GATES

Other books by Thurman C. Petty, Jr.:

Siege at the Eastern Gate:
The Story of Hezeziah and Sennacherib

Fire in the Gates:
The Drama of Jeremiah and the Fall of Judah

Gate of the Gods:
God's Quest for Nebuchadnezzar

The Open Gates:
From Babylon's Ashes, Freedom for the Jews

To order,
call
1-800-765-6955.

Visit us at
www.reviewandherald.com
for information on other Review and Herald® products.

THE
TEMPLE GATES

Josiah and the Reformation of Judah

THURMAN C. PETTY, JR.

Autumn House® Publishing
www.autumnhousepublishing.com
A Division of **REVIEW AND HERALD® PUBLISHING**
Since 1861

Copyright © 2008 by Review and Herald® Publishing Association

Published by Autumn House® Publishing, a division of Review and Herald®
Publishing Association

Copyright @ 1988 by Pacific Press Publishing Association

The Review and Herald® Publishing Association publishes biblically based materials
for spiritual, physical, and mental growth and Christian discipleship.

The author assumes full responsibility for the accuracy of all facts and quotations as
cited in this book.

Texts credited to NIV are from the *Holy Bible, New International Version.*
Copyright © 1973, 1978, 1984, International Bible Society. Used by permission of
Zondervan Bible Publishers.

This book was
Edited by Gerald Wheeler
Designed by Trent Truman
Cover art by Thiago Lobo
Typeset: Bembo 11.5/13.5

PRINTED IN U.S.A.

12 11 10 09 08   5 4 3 2 1

Library of Congress Cataloging-in-Publication Data
Petty, Thurman C., 1940-   .
  The temple gates: Josiah and the reformation of Judah / Thurman C. Petty, Jr.
      p. cm.
  1. Josiah, King of Judah—Fiction. 2. Bible. O.T.—History of biblical events—
Fiction. I. Title.
  PS3566.E894T46 2008
  813'.54—dc22

                                          2007029174

ISBN 978-0-8127-0442-6

Dedication

To Jesus
Who is sufficient for our Salvation.
Jesus is Enough!

Contents

A Chronology of Josiah's Time

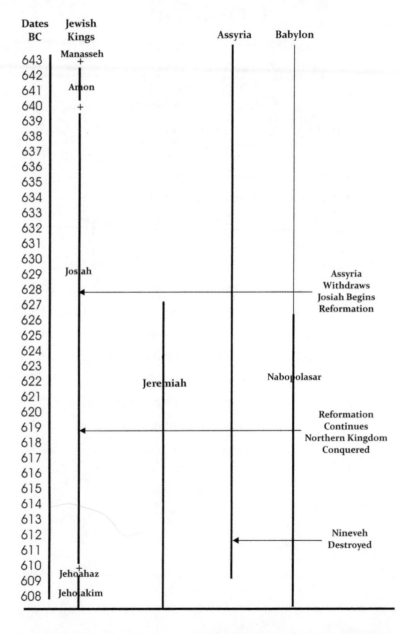

Dates BC	Jewish Kings		Assyria	Babylon	
643	Manasseh +				
642					
641	Amon				
640	+				
639					
638					
637					
636					
635					
634					
633					
632					
631					
630					
629	Josiah				Assyria
628					Withdraws
627					Josiah Begins Reformation
626					
625					
624					
623					
622		Jeremiah		Nabopolasar	
621					
620					Reformation
619					Continues
618					Northern Kingdom
617					Conquered
616					
615					
614					
613					
612					Nineveh
611					Destroyed
610	Jehoahaz +				
609					
608	Jehoiakim				

Jerusalem in the Time of Josiah
(Compiled from several maps by Thurman C. Petty, Jr.)

Tower of Hananel

Sheep Gate

Muster Gate

Upper Chamber of the Corner

Business Quarter

Fish Gate

East Gate

Temple Area

Gate of Ephraim

Horse Gate

Corner Gate

Water Gate

Upper Palace
(and courtyard prison)

Tower Over the Prison

Valley Gate

Solomon's Walls

VALLEY

CENTRAL VALLEY

Manasseh's Wall

Western Quarter

Old North Gate

Old Valley Gate

Hezekiah's Wall

Gihon Spring

Water Gate

City of David

Dung Gate

Lower Pool
Siloam

Hezekiah's Tunnel

Fountain Gate

VALLEY OF HINNOM

Old Pool (Reservoir)

Gate Between the Walls

KIDRON

Chapter 1

The King Is Dead! . . . Long Live the King!

"Where are you going?" As the sun began to brighten the horizon with a wash of pale light, the man sitting beside the warming flames of the cooking fire in the courtyard of his house glanced up from tightening the flint blade of his sickle.

"Up to the high place of Baal," his swarthy friend replied as he stood in the courtyard doorway. "Want to come along?"

"I believe I will," the first man agreed, laying down the sickle beside him. "We need Baal's help to ensure a good harvest."

The two strode up the stairway to Market Street, turned left, and made their way through the market as merchants began to set up their shops. Leaving the market area, they descended through the curves of East Street and exited the city through the East Gate.

"Too many people in Jerusalem, don't you think?" the first man observed.

"I agree. A lot of people have moved in from the countryside. They think it might be safer in the city."

"True. There've been lots of attacks and looting from bandits of late."

The men climbed the slope of the Mount of Olives and soon reached the high place of Baal. The sun peaked over the eastern hills. They faced the sun, knelt with their toes pointing behind them, then sat down on their heels. The ritual had already started.

The priests of Baal prostrated themselves before the altar. Perched on its top was a small gold-covered image of Baal holding a lightning bolt while standing on the figure of a bull. The bolt of lightning symbolized his control of the vital rainstorms, and the bull represented his power of fertility. As the cult prophets chanted they quickly slid into an ecstatic state that soon spread among the rest of the worshippers.

Manasseh had led his people into a spiritual bottomland. The son of Hezekiah had become fascinated with the gods of his grandfather Ahaz, rather than Yahweh, the Creator of heaven and earth, whom his father had been faithful to. Instead, Manasseh served the gods of the Canaanites, who had been dispossessed by his ancient ancestors. He set up altars to Baal and Ashtoreth, and even burned his own son in the Molech Tophet fire pit. The king consulted mediums and witches, and, though he did not outlaw the worship of Yahweh, he persecuted those who remained loyal to the God of Abraham, Isaac, and Jacob. So the worship of God had to go underground.

One of the first individuals that Manasseh murdered was the great prophet Isaiah. Tradition claims that the king had the prophet placed into a hollow log, and then ordered it sawn in half. Thus he ended the life of one who had, for nearly 50 years, spoken against evil and preached the true worship of Yahweh. Manasseh hunted down every prophet or spiritual leader of Yahweh and systematically murdered them, so that it came to be said that he had filled Jerusalem with blood.

The King Is Dead! . . . Long Live the King!

A woman climbed the steps that clung to the side of her house in the Western Quarter. On the roof her husband already knelt toward the east, his arms extended with his palms facing up. She joined him. They mumbled the lines of an ancient poem as they gazed at the myriads of points of light that peppered the night sky.

"Has your star group appeared yet?" the woman asked quietly. "Mine has climbed high into the sky. The one with the tail. Some call it the 'Great Bear.'"

"I've never seen a bear."

"Nor have I," the woman replied. "Notice that grouping of stars. Do you think someone somewhere might worship it?"

"Probably. But quiet now. Let us give our attention to our god—in the heavens."

Manasseh built altars to the sun god Shamash and the moon god Sin, and set up other idols in both courts of the Yahweh's Jerusalem Temple. He erected an Asherah pole in the Temple court and turned the rooms—set aside for the priests of Yahweh—over to male and female cult prostitutes. Thus those who came to worship Ashtoreth did so with the help of one or the other of these cult prostitutes. Sex in worship reminded the gods to maintain fertility for crops and animals, as well as for humans.

A young man stood on the steps of the Temple, examining the structure. *I've always been fascinated by that building,* he thought. *They say the Creator of heaven and earth lives in there. Why don't we see Him, the way we can Baal and the calf that King Jeroboam made in Bethel?*

Just then the youth turned to see a friend approaching him. He studied the man's expensive-looking clothing. "I swear by the name of Yahweh, Lord of heaven and earth, that I've not seen anyone who dresses better than you. That must be the new robe you told me about."

"That it is," the other replied, consciously modeling the expensive garment for anyone who passed. "I really got it for a bargain. A novice merchant from Babylon didn't really know the value of the wares he sold. Marvelous man. I'll have to see him again and discover what else lurks within his many trunks."

"I'll have to visit him too," the younger man said. "I swear by the god Molech, you did make a steal. I wonder what I could find."

The two climbed the remainder of steps and entered the Temple courtyard. Each passed the treasury and dropped a few pieces of silver bar into the receptacle, and went to kneel at their usual spot. There they worshipped the altar and the offering, praying to them as though they were gods in and of themselves.

Following the completion of the evening sacrifice, the worshippers were about to rise when someone stepped forward, dressed in camel's hair with a leather belt around his waist. Everyone recognized him as a prophet. Later they learned that his name was Zephaniah.

"Thus says the Lord." His voice carried easily across the courtyard. "'I will stretch out my hand against Judah and against all who live in Jerusalem. I will cut off from this place every remnant of Baal, the names of the pagan and the idolatrous priests—those who bow down on the roofs to worship the starry host, those who bow down and swear by the Lord and who also swear by Molech, those who turn back from following the Lord and neither seek the Lord nor inquire of him. Be silent before the Sovereign Lord, for the day of the Lord is near. The Lord has prepared a sacrifice; he has consecrated those he has invited. On the day of the Lord's sacrifice I will punish the princes and the king's sons and all those clad in foreign clothes. On that day I will punish all who avoid stepping on the threshold, who fill the temple of their gods with violence and deceit.'"*

The prophet seemed to have more to say, but suddenly stopped, turned, and strode out the side gate of the Temple. He disappeared before the royal guards could catch him.

The two friends looked at each other awkwardly. "I think he had us in mind," the first gasped, swallowing hard.

"What do you mean?"

"Just before we came in here I took an oath by the Lord, and only a sentence or two later one in the name of Molech."

"And I'm wearing foreign clothes." The second man thought for a moment. "But I don't see anything wrong with wearing clothes made in Babylon."

For several years Manasseh remained a faithful vassal of Assyria, paying tribute to Judah's great enemy. Throughout his reign the people increasingly resented their idolatrous king. In order to quiet the unrest, Manasseh decided to break his treaty with Assyria and assert his independence, as his father had done. At the end of the year he declined to pay the regular tribute demanded by his overlords.

"I think I'll go to worship at the shrine at Bethel," the king announced one day. "I believe that there I will receive greater power over my subjects."

"I don't think that's a good idea," one of his counselors cautioned. "The Assyrians control that territory, and even though we haven't seen any sign of them along our borders for some time, it seems to me it would be too risky to go there."

"Nonsense," Manasseh grumbled. "The gods will protect me from anyone who attempts to harm me."

And, true to his word, Manasseh and a bodyguard of 100 soldiers left Jerusalem and traveled north 20 miles to Bethel. The king approached the altar that stood before the golden calf and stood hands raised in prayer as the smoke of his incense curled toward the heavens.

"Assyrians!" one of his guards suddenly shouted. "Battle ranks!"

Manasseh's guards sprang into action and charged the small Assyrian platoon that advanced toward them. The skirmish lasted only minutes, however, as Judahite soldiers were no match for the veteran troops of Nineveh. Those who did not fall by the sword retreated in all directions, leaving Manasseh standing, alone, by the altar.

The Assyrians bound him with chains, took away his royal robes and sandals, and, forced him to follow their chariots 800 miles to the jewel of the Assyrian Empire—Babylon. There they imprisoned him in a dungeon.

Days, weeks, months passed, and the stale bread and putrid water began to wear on his idolatrous heart. The stench of urine and the nauseous smell of feces sickened him. There seemed to be no way of escape. No one in Babylon cared about him, and none of his gods came to his aid.

Gradually Manasseh began to remember his father. Hezekiah had worshipped Yahweh faithfully, and even though he had suffered because of some of his own wrongdoing, Yahweh had come to his assistance. Once the Lord God had destroyed the Assyrian army in a single night. And He had healed a deadly boil, and caused the shadow of a sundial to go backward. Yahweh did all that for Hezekiah. And Manasseh, his son, had turned his back on the God of his people, choosing, instead, to worship impotent pagan gods.

One day the captive monarch began to weep. Tears ran down his cheeks and soaked his beard. Hour after hour he pleaded with Yahweh. "I have no reason to expect any help from You," he acknowledged, holding his hands upward, palms up, begging for the blessing of Yahweh, but bowing his head, feeling unworthy even to look to heaven. "I have sinned in worshipping other gods. I've killed scores of Your innocent people. I filled the streets of Jerusalem with blood—forgive me, Yahweh. Forgive me and help me."

Eventually a peace settled over him. His cell seemed to lighten a bit; the air smelled fresher than it had for months. "Thank You, Lord," he finally exclaimed. "If I spend the rest of my days here, I'm grateful for Your forgiveness and Your peace."

The sounds of laughter and the shouts of children filled the garden as Josiah and his friends frolicked together among the trees and shrubs. One of the boys had a stick and was beating a rhythm from a popular tune while other boys imitated dances they had seen at the festivals. They wore the traditional *kethoneth* [shirt] that hung to their knees. The woolen garments swayed as they moved about in time with the drum.

Old King Manasseh sat on a bench nearby, smiling. He enjoyed the antics of his grandson, Josiah, and the child's friends. One of the greatest blessings grandparents received came from watching their grandchildren play.

The Assyrians had released Manasseh from his dungeon in Babylon, and, after having him swear allegiance to their empire, they sent him back to Judah to be king once more. Returning to his capital city, Manasseh spent the rest of his life working to undo the spiritual damage he had caused in Judah. He removed most of the high places, and directed the people to the Temple in Jerusalem as the only place they could worship Yahweh.

And yet the people had become wedded to their idols

during the more than 50 years of Manasseh's reign. Now they resisted his reforms. The repentant king was old, and few seemed to take him seriously.

He watched the dancing of the boys for an hour or more before he felt a pain in his chest. The throbbing grew within, and the stabbing pain caused him to gasp. The stricken man stumbled into the house, agony etched on his face. Making it into his bedchamber, he collapsed on his couch facedown.

A palace slave sprang to Manasseh's side. Pulling the king up onto the bed, he tried to make him comfortable. Only then did the servant realize that his monarch had died. He began a lament for the dead. Others heard it and rushed to the royal bedchamber to witness the sight.

"We'd better let the people know." Shaphan, though young, filled one of the highest offices in the government—that of palace scribe.

Messengers immediately sprang into action and fanned out over the city and into the countryside. "The king is dead; the king is dead. Long live the king." It sounded strange to speak of life in the same breath as death, but the ancient phrase somehow brought comfort.

Wailing filled the city of Jerusalem. People collected at the palace gate, mourning. Many had torn their robes and put ashes onto their heads. Some were professional mourners and hoped to receive payment. Others came because they thought that it was just the right thing to do. Still others were merely curious. A few genuinely grieved, anticipating what would happen when Crown Prince Amon became king.

Josiah pushed through the crowd that had gathered near the bedchamber, wanting to see his grandfather. He slipped through the people milling in the hallway.

"Josiah." The boy recognized his mother's voice and turned to see her reach out for his hand. "Come with me. We can't go in there now. They're preparing his body for burial."

The King Is Dead! . . . Long Live the King!

Jedidah tugged her son's hand and led him to his own bedchamber. She appeared to be anguished . . . frightened, even. "We need to stay out of the way until they're finished." Then she stared out of the window that opened onto the garden, where minutes before the boy had known nothing but delight. "They'll be ready soon."

The king's body rested on a bier in the palace garden while those who desired filed by to get a last look at their fallen monarch.

Jedidah led her son Josiah by the bier, and the boy reached out and put his hand on the folded hands of his grandfather. He had known only the gentle, God-fearing final years of the king. But now he was gone.

Manasseh had reigned 55 years, 45 since the death of his father, Hezekiah. Most people in the land had known no other ruler. Many couldn't fathom what it would be like to have anyone else as king.

When the last of the mourners had left, the palace servants carried the body down the path to the family tomb and placed it into the chamber that had been hollowed out in the hillside. According to ancient custom the dead were buried, as far as possible, the same day they died.

After sealing the tomb, the officials departed, leaving behind two guards to see that no one would pilfer the grave. "He led me to Yahweh," Jedidah said to her son. "I hope you become as good a king as your grandfather . . . after God changed his heart."

---

* Zephaniah 1:4-9, NIV.

Chapter 2

Blades Flash in the Night

Josiah wandered through the palace from room to room, looking for his father, King Amon. The boy peered into the throne room, but Amon was not there. He stuck his head into the council chamber, but it also was empty. Going down the hall, Josiah glanced into the king's bedchamber. But again, his father was not there. Finally the boy stopped a servant hurrying to deliver a message. "Where's Father?" the child asked, racing after him. "Have you seen the king?"

"No, but he usually goes to the Temple about this time of day . . . to worship at the Ashtoreth shrine."

"In the Temple?"

"Yes, your grandfather set up the shrine several years ago. He took it down, but King Amon replaced it."

"Do you know where Mother is?" Josiah continued to glance into one door and then another.

"Yes," the servant answered, for he had just delivered a message to her, and received one in return. "She's in her chambers."

"Thank you." Josiah turned and jogged down the long hall toward the rooms in which his mother lived. The king had lost interest in her several years before, when he had become immersed in reviving the various religions that his father had destroyed in his later years. One of them had cult prostitutes with whom a man could worship the goddess of

20

fertility. Amon regularly participated in its rites.

The king knew of his wife's faithfulness to Yahweh, and it angered him. "Why did my father yoke me together with one of '*those*' people?" he often muttered. "Why couldn't he have gotten me a wife who worships the way I do?" The Ashtoreth cult had its male counterparts as well.

"Mother?" Josiah entered her chambers and found Jedidah resting on a bench.

"Yes, Josiah." She smiled as she saw her son. *He'll make a fine king one day*, she thought.

"The servant said that Father's at the Temple worshipping at the Ashtoreth shrine." He gazed into his mother's face. "Why did he put a pagan shrine in Yahweh's Temple?"

Tears welled up in her hazel eyes. "I don't know, son. It seems that he wants to erase everything good about being one of God's people. He encourages all the people to worship at the high places and shrines." She wiped her eyes with a linen cloth. "We'll just have to pray and hope that God preserves our nation until someone sets it straight."

"Tell me again about when you were a little girl." Josiah always enjoyed hearing about his mother's childhood.

"I grew up in the town of Bozkath, down on the Shephelah—the western slope of the central highlands." Drawing her son close to her, she rested her chin on his head. She always liked the smell of his hair.

"We didn't live far from Lachish—about three miles— and we often went to the market there to purchase the things we needed. But the thing I remember most was running through the olive groves just before the sun came up, and then watching its golden disc rise and sparkle in the heavy dew on the leaves and in the grass." She stared into space, remembering.

"But I had to hurry back for morning prayers," Jedidah continued. "We always had prayers at daybreak and again at dusk. My father and mother loved Yahweh and couldn't understand why people wanted to worship idols that can't see or hear." She paused. "And I loved to go up on the hill behind the house and look out over the valley below. If I squinted my eyes enough on a clear day, I could see the Great Sea [the Mediterranean]."

"Were you happy about becoming a princess?" Josiah took in every word and pictured his mother doing the things she told him about.

"Oh, yes." She beamed. "Every girl dreams of becoming a princess." Tears formed at the corner of her eyes. "But I was very disappointed that they married me to Amon." She remembered the day. "He's very good-looking and seemed so wonderful at first. I really loved him." Again she dabbed at her eyes with the linen cloth. "But then he became enthralled with witchcraft and idolatry. I wouldn't go to the shrines with him. Soon he didn't have any time for me.

"And when he became king, it got even worse. I hardly know him anymore. But you shouldn't worry about such things," she added, starting to rise. "One day you will be king, and I hope you will worship Yahweh and lead our nation back to God."

"I will, Mother. I will."

Two years passed, and King Amon became more and more idolatrous. He scarcely had time for affairs of state. The nation drifted like a flock without a shepherd. It had no judge to make the final decisions on important cases or warrior to lead the army into battle.

"We've got to do something," growled the chief counselor as the palace steward poured wine into his fine pottery cup. The royal council met in a side room off the throne room. "The Assyrians and the Babylonians are at war. Ashuruballit is calling in all his forces from the colonies in order to protect the homeland. Where do we stand in all of this? Will Judah continue as a nation, or will we be swallowed up by someone else?"

"I saw the Assyrians leave the border areas north of Judah last month," one of the generals commented. "It's been a welcome relief to my men."

"If only King Amon would take charge of things," the prime minister remarked. "Perhaps we would have someone to steer us through this. But he spends his time at the Temple, doing . . . you know what."

"Do you remember Joash?" the head scribe asked. "He was only 7 years old when he began to reign, and with proper counsel . . ."

"I see what you mean," the general cut him off and held up his hand. "The walls sometimes have 'ears,' and one has to be careful what one says. The chopping block or the hanging tree always has room for one more treasonous official."

The council froze for a moment, but soon continued with their meeting.

The palace steward blanched at what he had just heard, and slipped though the door to the royal kitchens. He summoned his assistant, and they withdrew into a workroom.

"The counselors are talking about . . ."

The assistant raised his hand. "You know we are bound to secrecy on anything we hear in the palace. You cannot divulge what you hear in there."

"Yes, yes. I know." The steward became agitated. "But they're beginning to talk about how much better the kingdom would be if Josiah were to become king. They referred to Joash . . ."

"They can't do that!" his assistant boomed, then suddenly became quieter, realizing that they might be heard. "They're the most important men of the government. We need them. If they get involved in a plot against the king, it could destroy all of us."

"They'll be executed." The steward had already decided what he must do. "We've got to do it for them before they do it themselves." The official suddenly shivered.

His assistant's face grew white as he realized that such an act would guarantee him a short life. "Are you sure this has to be done?"

"Positive! You know how he treats the palace staff. And the Temple priests . . . and the people as a whole." The steward paced the floor. "I don't like this any more than you do. I love life, and I'm doing just what I always wanted to do." He hissed out the words. "But I can't allow the king to destroy the whole nation!"

"Sounds to me as if you have enough anger within you to drive you to this," his assistant observed. "But now you have a more urgent reason—to save the council from an act that would lead to their doom." He thought a moment. "How and when shall . . . ?"

"Let's do it tonight." The steward's voice rang with finality. "If we wait, word might slip out, and we might fail."

In the early hours before daybreak, the darkest part of the night, two figures dressed in black, their faces smeared with charcoal, slipped down the passageway toward the royal bedchamber. The guard stood beside the door, sleeping at his post.

He'll die for this if anyone discovers he was sleeping, the chief steward thought. *With any luck, though, we can do our business so quietly that he'll never know we've been here.*

The two stewards had been here before—many times. They moved into position, and two blades flashed in the darkness. The king made no sound . . . he was dead. Slipping past the still-sleeping guard, they made their way out the servants' entrance and vanished into the night. *The king is dead,* the chief steward told himself. *Long live the king!*

The steady drizzle kept almost everyone away. They hadn't liked the king anyway, so why should they attend a wet funeral. Jedidah and Josiah stood beside the bier for a long time.

Jedidah wept. *I really loved him, but he died to me long ago,* she thought to herself.

"It was terrible, what they did to Father." His hot tears mingled with the cold rain as it coursed down his cheeks. "Whoever is the next king needs to find out who did this, and have them brought to justice."

"You'll be the next king," Jedidah replied softly. "And you will see that the murderers are caught, given a fair trial, and, if found guilty, executed."

"Me? King?" Josiah erupted. The thought had never really struck him before. He knew that tradition required that the next king be the son of the fallen monarch. "What will I do? I . . ." Then his voice fell as he realized the presence of others. His mother squeezed his hand, as much as to say: *Be quiet. There'll be plenty of time to talk about this.*

Those carrying the bier placed the king into the family tomb beside his father, closed the grave, and marched away, not even leaving a guard at the tomb.

"Let's go inside, Josiah. Tomorrow you will sit on David's throne." She took his hand and smiled, and the two retreated into the palace.

Chapter 3

The Coronation

"This is the most important convocation you've ever attended," Jedidah instructed as she helped her son into his new royal attire. "It's a very solemn time—it's not playtime."

"I–I know that, Mother." The boy had never stuttered before, and he shivered as he thought of the challenge before him. "You'll be nearby, won't you?"

"Yes, but you'll have to climb the stairs to the throne by yourself. I can't stand by you when they anoint you and put the crown on your head." His mother masked her great fear for the future of her son. How could an 8-year-old boy, even with an adult regent to guide him, run a country whose national economy, government, and religion lay in a tangled mess? "More than anything else, Josiah . . . more than anything else, be true to Yahweh. Don't go with the counselors or wise men to any of the shrines, or allow them to turn you from your allegiance to God. We've been over this before."

"I have given my life to Yahweh," the boy assured her, "just as you taught me." Josiah stood to his full height, straight as a plumb line. "I will not let any man lead me from Him. I will be true to God, no matter what the cost!"

The palace buzzed with activity as the servants hurried to make the final preparations for the feast that would follow the coronation. All the king's advisors and nobles from all over Judah would be joining the festivities, so every detail needed to be in order.

Where are the chief steward and his assistant? the servants wondered to themselves. They had always depended upon the pair to supervise such affairs. Their absence seemed inexcusable. *Perhaps they're needed to supervise preparations in another part of the city,* some wondered. Still their frustration began to transform into anger.

"There are a lot of people here," a woman half whispered to her husband as they sought to enter the Temple complex.

"Yes, there are," her husband replied. "I'll be happy when the rituals are finished and we go to the feast at the palace."

"I agree, but it's best not to speak of it now. Others might get the idea that food is more important than a king."

"Well, isn't it? At least it's better than the last king we had."

His wife had to stifle outright laughter.

Most in attendance wore the *kethoneth,* a shirtlike garment. Some hung to the knees, while others went as far as the ankles. All bore the blue tassels* required of every Jew. The air reeked with the odors of human sweat and the pungent perfumes that the people used to mask the stench. A few of the wealthy women wore close-fitting garments of linen, imported from Egypt. Red and white seemed to be the predominant colors. Most women had used cosmetics of various sorts, some to enlarge the eyes by blackening the eyelashes, and others had applied an additional red-blush coloring on their cheeks.

When the royal party marched out through the palace gates, thousands of voices cheered. Josiah and Jedidah led the royal family, government leaders, scribes, nobles, and servants. She looked down with joy at her son. Only her love for her Creator exceeded her fondness for him. Soon he would be king, and she would be the queen mother—a position almost as powerful as that of the king himself. And for many years to come she would be his chief counselor.

She remembered her father joyfully reenacting the tales of Yahweh's triumphs on behalf of Israel. But she returned to the present when she saw the Temple gates. The procession entered, and the official Levite heralds sounded the ram's horns. The shrill blast of a dozen horns trembled above the shouting of the multitude, and those who hadn't already found a place, elbowed their way into the Temple's outer court.

The coronation would take place on the Temple porch, for the new king needed Yahweh's blessing. For generations the people had worshipped pagan deities at the many high places throughout the country. Yet tradition still bound them by slender cords to the one true God—Yahweh, Creator of all. And according to tradition, a new king was always anointed and crowned beside "Boaz," the large bronze pillar that stood on the north side of the Temple porch.

A hush fell over the throng as Josiah climbed the Temple steps, accompanied by the high priest and the prime minister—the highest official of the government. The boy stood straight, and as tall as he could, beside the giant bronze pillar, a solemn expression on his face. He peered at the high priest. The white priestly robes that hung to his feet, the multicolored breastplate, and the turban on his head, all gave the religious leader a stately appearance.

Jedidah proudly waited at the foot of the stairs. Except for the absence of the crown and signet ring—which rested on an orate pillow held by one of the priests—Josiah was dressed as a king. *I can hardly wait to see the crown upon his head,* she thought.

The boy looked over the crowd while he waited for the ceremony to begin. Everyone had dressed in his or her finest clothing. Many women wore a veillike shawl that dropped to their knees. Most of the wealthy women seemed heavy with jewelry: earrings, necklaces, bands of gold around the ankles, gold rings in their noses, dozens of bracelets on their arms, and gold threads running through their hair. Absently the boy wondered how they could possibly be comfortable with all those things hanging on them.

Josiah's attention abruptly stopped wandering when the high priest signaled for him to kneel beside the pillar. The high priest read Yahweh's law pertaining to the king. Then, handing the scroll to another priest, he slowly poured fragrant anointing oil onto the head of the crown prince. The oil ran down his cheeks and dripped off his nose, staining his beautiful robes. The high priest then set the crown upon his head.

The new king now arose and stood beside the bronze pillar, a smile on his face. The old priest's voice rang clear and strong: "I present to you . . . Josiah . . . king of Judah!" And the people thundered their praise: "Long live the king! Long live the king!" The chant echoed across Jerusalem.

The crowd then followed the royal party back to the palace, where Josiah climbed the six steps between the golden lions . . . and occupied the throne of David.

"Long live King Josiah!"

---

* See Numbers 15:38.

Chapter 4

The Trial

"I'm pleased that you've come," the boyish voice said from the golden throne. Its occupant's feet swung back and forth. His purple sandals matched his royal robe and turban.

The throne room measured somewhat larger than any other room in the palace, and perhaps that of any other building in Jerusalem. The enclosure had window openings to the outside on the two ends and on one side. They allowed the only exterior light, and, during the summer, permitted air to pass through the room to cool it. Shutters sealed out the cold and rain during the winter. With the shutters closed, olive oil lamps set on various stands around the room and in niches recessed in the walls illuminated the chamber.

Since the room had as its primary purpose the assembly of people before the king, it had no seats. Visitors, dignitaries from other countries, council members, criminals—all had to stand to the side of or in front of the throne.

Those who had assembled this day included the leaders of every important branch of government: the prime minister, who also acted as the royal cupbearer (he tasted the wine before it was served to the king to make sure it was not poisoned); the high priest; the commanding general of the army; Shaphan, the second priest and palace scribe; Joah, the recorder; the governor of Jerusalem, and several of the elders of the city and nation.

"We need to organize a search for the two men who assassinated my father," Josiah announced.

"How do you know it was two men?" The general sounded skeptical.

"My father's body had two wounds, and the guards found two knives. That's why I believe there are two men." Josiah seemed more mature than his years would suggest.

"That sounds reasonable," the prime minister acknowledged. "We should send the soldiers right now before the assassins get away."

"Agreed," the general seconded as he looked to Josiah for permission to proceed. At the young king's nod, the general left the room. He returned a few minutes later, a smile on his face. "I have given the orders," he announced.

"Who do you think could have done it?" Shaphan asked.

"Perhaps I can appoint the chief steward to look into it," Josiah suggested.

"Good idea," the prime minister nodded. "He knows the palace inside and out and ought to be able to find out who did it."

After the king had gone, the councilmen talked about him among themselves.

"Such wisdom in an 8-year-old!" Hilkiah, the high priest, commented.

"Perhaps he'll do well as king," Shaphan said.

"We can hope so," the prime minister sighed. "But we've got to keep a tight control on him, or he might mess up the national situation."

"What do you mean?" queried Joah, the royal recorder.

"He's a faithful believer in Yahweh, is he not?"

"Yes," Shaphan replied. "But what does that have to do with it?"

The prime minister put his finger to his lips, and then spoke quietly. "If he gets ideas about Yahweh being the *only* God, and tries to destroy the shrines and high places, he could upset the stability and thus the economy of the country."

"Yes, he could," Joah agreed. "But remember how the economy grew in the days of Hezekiah? My grandfather Joah, who was also court recorder, told me that in spite of the wars with Assyria, Judah flourished. If King Josiah moves in that direction, I don't think it would unsettle the country all that much."

The prime minister scowled. "Well, we'll see."

After leaving the throne room, Josiah entered the family's personal quarters. The royal residence ranked as the largest house in Jerusalem, though it would be considered small by many people of other city-states, such as Nineveh and Babylon.

The entrance led into a small garden. Just inside the front door, to the left, off the hall, the family would greet visitors in the main sitting room. Unless they had been invited to stay as guests, such visitors generally went no further.

Behind the main sitting room lay the guest quarters, shut off from the royal residence by a double door. Down the hallway beyond the doors lay several suites, with two to three rooms each, one for the king, one for the queen, and one for the queen mother. Lesser wives and others would occupy additional rooms as space allowed.

A larger room in the center of the bedchambers doubled as a dining room and a gathering place for the family. Behind it and tucked into the courtyard was the kitchen, with a wood-burning pit overlaid by an iron grating. Storage rooms held grain and other foodstuffs, water storage jars, and dishes and pans.

Behind the courtyard was an area employed for the butchering of animals for food. With no refrigeration, people had learned that the best way to keep meat fresh involved keeping it on the hoof until needed.

At the corner of the palace, with no access from the royal

residence, stood a tower with a dungeon beneath it. Prisoners not thought to be a threat were kept in barracks-like buildings in its courtyard.

Josiah's mother stood just inside the door of the royal quarters. As soon as he entered, she threw her arms around him and squeezed him tightly. "I worried that you would be afraid of dealing with such high dignitaries," she said when she released him from her hug.

"I am king," Josiah said solemnly. "I must do the work of a king." He paused and looked into his mother's eyes. "Of course, I shall need much counsel from you and others." Josiah kicked off his sandals, as he preferred to go barefoot. "What should we do when they find the ones who killed Father?"

"They should receive a fair trial." Jedidah looked through her window at people entering the Temple through the main gate. "And I fear that we'll know them well when they are brought for trial."

"Didn't Father hold court down by the East Gate?"

"Yes, that's the proper place to do it. That way everyone will know the outcome of the trial. But many kings hold court before their throne."

"Should I act as the judge, or should I defer to an older man of superior wisdom?"

"That will be up to you. You are king."

"They've got them, they've got them." The shout rose from people on every side as the soldiers entered the Sheep Gate leading the accused. The men had their arms bound behind their backs, yet walked without any urging from the soldiers. As though they had expected this to happen, they held their heads high and refused to cower.

"We should thank them rather than hang them," the

prime minister whispered. "If they hadn't done it, some-one else would have."

"That may be true," Joah hissed back, "but the less we talk about it, the better."

"Isn't that the chief steward and his assistant?" the prime minister asked. He grimaced, thinking how close he and the others of the inner council had come to assassinating Amon themselves. "Who do you think will judge the case?"

No one answered as the elders hurried in the direction of the East Gate.

"How can we try the case?" Josiah asked. "There are no witnesses. It took place at night, and the guard must have been sleeping." (A guard who slept on duty could be exe-cuted, but this seemed to have been overlooked in the pres-ent case.) "He doesn't remember anyone entering or leaving the room."

"I think, perhaps," the boy-king's mother suggested, "that you'd better let one of the more experienced men han-dle this case. It will show wisdom on your part, and you can learn from watching the trial."

"Well spoken," Josiah replied, echoing what he had heard others in the court say.

As he and Jedidah headed toward the East Gate, people parted to let them through, smiling as they passed. Arriving at the place, Josiah sat down on the bench that served as the judgment seat.

"This case is difficult and requires one of superior wis-dom and experience," Josiah spoke in a commanding though immature voice. "The one I've chosen"—he indicated the man who stood beside him—"has a long and distinguished record of defending truth, and has shown fairness to all con-cerned." He stood to his feet. "I recommend that the men be handed over to the jailers while the judge and his assistants have time to examine the case."

"Good thinking," a woman whispered to her companion. "Most new rulers would conduct such a trial themselves to persuade people that they were in control."

"But Josiah has demonstrated his wisdom by stepping aside," her friend commented. "I like him."

"We don't have any witnesses to the murder of Amon," Joah pointed out. "How can we condemn the men without any witnesses? The only evidence we have against them is that they fled. But they might have had some less-criminal reason for leaving Jerusalem."

"Technically, you're right," the prime minister acknowledged. "But that is not the only circumstantial evidence that points to them as the culprits. It all depends upon what the judge decides."

"And King Josiah surely chose the right judge," Shaphan added. "He has the most honorable reputation in all Judah."

The trial moved forward with, as expected, no actual witnesses to point the finger at the accused. But many other things indicated that the chief steward and his assistant had been the assassins. The two lived in the palace, which gave them access to the royal bedchamber. The guard admitted he had been asleep for a period of time during the night. The murder weapons had come from the palace kitchen. One cook recalled hearing the sound of arguing coming from the chief steward's office the day before. Both the chief steward and his assistant had been absent from their duties the following morning. And a military patrol had stumbled across them hiding in an abandoned tomb in the Kidron Valley.

The judge took time to consider each piece of evidence, and to those near the front of the crowd, it was obvious that he was putting it all together in his head. He asked many questions of the various witnesses. When all the information regarding the assassination had been presented, and the judge had asked his last question, the crowd quietly awaited his verdict.

The official sat thinking for a long time. Occasionally he would ask about an item that witnesses had presented, and nodded his head as much as to say, "Yes, I remember that now." At last he rose to his feet, his decision made.

"I find that the accused men are guilty. Every evidence points to them. Chief steward, and assistant chief steward, did you or did you not kill King Amon?"

The two men stood before the judge, heads down in an attitude of hopelessness. "Yes, Your Honor," the chief steward finally acknowledged. "We are the ones who killed King Amon. We are guilty."

A sudden intake of breath throughout the assembly showed surprise at the judgment, even though everyone seemed to have been expecting that the culprits were guilty. Then a collective exhale sounded more like a sigh of relief.

Later in the day passersby could see two bodies hanging outside the East Gate. The chief steward and his assistant had sealed their "sacrifice" by their own deaths. But no one ever knew that the king's own council had itself discussed such drastic action, or that the assassins had given their lives to spare the lives of the leaders of the country.

Chapter 5

The Marriage

"But Your Majesty," pleaded the prime minister, "you don't understand. The people of Judah already worship Yahweh."

The council room buzzed with a mixture of anger, surprise, agreement, and delight. The room itself could seat perhaps 25 comfortably. Though somewhat plain, its walls had been painted with various patterns of grapes, pomegranates, and other designs, all applied in carefully aligned rows. The benches on which the councilmen sat provided little comfort to the men who occupied them. The king occupied a thronelike chair positioned on a platform raised a half cubit above the floor. It provided him much better support than his counselors enjoyed.

The members of the council included the prime minister; Hilkiah, the high priest; the commanding general of the army; several elders from various cities of the kingdom; the scribe Shaphan, the second priest and secretary of the council; and Ahikam, son of Shaphan, and the youngest member of the group.

"I know that what you are saying is true," Josiah responded. "Yet they cling to their idols as well."

The king, now 13, clearly realized the spiritual condition of his people, and what Yahweh required of them.

"I don't think you could label them as idols," another counselor protested. "They are just, ah, visible objects that help us to experience the presence of God."

The Temple Gates

"And which god are you worshipping at these shrines?" the king questioned.

"Well, ah . . ."

"See why I stand true to Yahweh." The young king pointed at the group, speaking sternly. "The shrines and high places at which you worship have nothing to do with Yahweh. They are sites where the people serve Baal, Ashtoreth, and other deities."

Josiah paused for a moment, his eyes ablaze. "I will remain true to Yahweh, and Him only shall I serve. And I appeal to you to join me, so that God will be able to bless our nation."

The grumbling council members rose and shuffled out of the room. Josiah remained on his council room throne for a long time, thinking of the recent exchange, and wanting desperately to do something to bring his subjects back to the blessings they could receive by worshipping the one true God—Yahweh.

Josiah had reigned for only five years, and it was understood that he was under the control of his mother, but of late he had been making his own decisions. In the eyes of the law he was now a man. And he had learned his lessons well in regard to rulership, having gained a good grasp of statesmanship as well as how to size up officials, discovering whom to trust and whom to watch closely. He respected his council, even though they had occasional theological disagreements regarding which gods the people worshipped.

Jedidah and Josiah, mother and son, went twice a day to the Temple to worship God as they observed the morning and evening sacrifice. In spite of the fact that pagan trappings adorned much of the Temple, the priests still went through the paces of the Temple service—even though their hearts felt no real union with Yahweh. But those who truly desired to worship Yahweh still received a blessing.

The Marriage

One day as the king and his mother passed through the Royal Gate on the way back to the palace, Josiah seemed more meditative than usual.

"What are you thinking about, my son?"

"I'm disturbed by the idolatry practiced in the Temple." The two paused and glanced back into the Temple court. "The priests not only give their permission for these shrines to be in God's Temple, but they take money from those who worship, by also serving as priests in these shrines!" Josiah grew more and more agitated as he continued. "They even misuse the rooms set aside for other priests to stay in when they come to serve in the Temple. The priests have turned those chambers into the abodes of the cult prostitutes!"

"I'm aware of that." Jedidah's voice quivered. "Your father spent much time worshipping at the Ashtoreth shrine with them." Her voice grew more bitter. "If he'd paid more attention to Yahweh's ways, he'd still be alive today. But then," she paused, "I wouldn't have had you as my king, would I?"

Josiah ignored her comment. "Do you think I should use my power as king to remove these offenses to Yahweh?"

"Yes, Josiah." She paused. "But not yet. People still haven't learned to trust you as their king. You are only 13, and it would be hard for many to take someone so young seriously."

The king smiled. "I will cleanse the Temple. But I guess I'll just have to wait."

"A good decision," she replied as they turned again toward the palace.

Shaphan sat in the palace garden speaking with King Josiah. "You've been faithful to Yahweh from the time you became king—at the age of 8."

"That's true."

"Why?"

"Yahweh is creator of heaven and earth. He created me
. . . and you. Then too, I've read the records. God blessed
Judah during the reign of my great-grandfather, Hezekiah,"
the young man explained. "And I've read about the wickedness of my grandfather Manasseh. Even though he came back
to Yahweh in his later years, still the country refused to follow him." Josiah rested his chin on the back of his hand.
"And I saw the results of the idolatry of my father." An angry
expression clouded his face. "If he'd followed Yahweh, he'd
still be alive today."

"I see."

Josiah's eyes narrowed, and his voice became more firm.
"As I see it, our only hope of survival as a nation lies in a total
return to Yahweh." The king stared at the shrine on the top of
the Mount of Olives. "Our only hope is to destroy all the pagan
shrines and high places, and cleanse the Temple once and for
all. The only way we can survive is to come back to Yahweh."

"That's not likely to happen," Shaphan said as he stood
to leave.

"Why not?"

"The people are wedded to their idols. You'd have to
become a very strong king to carry out what you've suggested."

The next day Jedidah spoke with her son about marriage.

"Do you really think I'm old enough to get married?"
Josiah felt appalled by his mother's suggestion.

The queen mother revealed that she and Shaphan had
taken it upon themselves to choose a wife for him. "It's very
important for you to have a male child who will take your
place on the throne should you die," she explained. "Your
father and I were married when we were 15, and it's a good
thing, because you were born when I was 16. Otherwise, you
wouldn't have been old enough to become king."

They stood in the main sitting room with Shaphan.

"I see," the king said. "And if I marry her, I shall love her?" Josiah motioned for the others to sit down.

"Yes, Josiah," his mother responded. "When we marry, we learn to love each other. It's so important for the parents, or someone who knows the children very well—I say, it's so important to let older people who know you choose a spouse for you. It would be a mistake for a young man to make such a lifelong decision by himself."

"And a king is expected to have several wives," Shaphan, who had so far remained silent, now explained.

"Why didn't Father have other wives?"

"Your father was still quite young." Jedidah paled. "And he spent so much with the fertility cults that . . ." Tears streamed down her face. "I loved him so much! But he never really gave himself a chance to love me." She wiped her eyes.

"We've already made the arrangements," Shaphan resumed. "She's beautiful, she's intelligent, she's witty, and she's 13 too."

"Who is she? What family does she come from?"

"Her name is Zebidah, the daughter of Pedaiah, and she comes from Rumah, about 12 miles west of the Sea of Chinnereth.[1] I'm sure you'll love her."

"Zebidah." Josiah let the name roll off his tongue. "That's a pretty name."

"And she's a pretty young woman, too," his mother added.

The time for the wedding seemed to come sooner than expected. With so many things to do and so many arrangements to make, Jedidah and the palace servants kept busy from sunup to sunset. But at last they had everything ready. The bride had arrived from Rumah.

The Temple Gates

The bride's party had taken up residence in a nobleman's home not far from the palace. Zebidah and her servants had laid out her gowns for the festivities that evening.

"It's so exciting," one woman servant exclaimed. "You're going to be a queen!"

"Yes," Zebidah squealed. "I can hardly believe it. I hope he's handsome and charming . . ."

Another servant worked on Zebidah's long black hair, brushing it and adding ointment to produce a glassy sheen. "I'm going to braid part of your hair," she managed to say between the ivory hairpins she held in her mouth. "I'll weave strips of gold and silver into the strands." Besides that, she inserted pearls and other beautiful stones into the braids. "I'm going to leave most of the hair free, so it'll flow down over your shoulders."

"That's a good idea," Zebidah said. "That way my hair will become part of my dress. I like that." Between giggles, the servant wound another braid around the bride's temples, giving the appearance of a wreath encircling her head.

"Hold still now," the girl in charge of the makeup teased. "I'm going to work on your face."

"How can you make that any better?" the bride-to-be mocked. "Nothing I've ever tried to do made me look better. I'm a marred lump of clay, and I'm likely to stay that way."

"Ha, ha," her hairdresser teased. "You're beautiful, and you know it. She's just going to make a jewel look even more desirable."

"I'm going to use kohl[2] around your eyes," the servant explained. "It will make them appear larger."

"Nothing like big eyes to charm a man!" laughed the girl braiding Zebidah's hair observed.

"Don't make fun," Zebidah protested. "If you think it will help, then make them as big as you can."

"I'll use iron red ochre on your cheeks and lips and henna on your fingernails and toenails," added the woman doing her makeup. "That will add color to your complexion. Then I'll use creams and ointments and mix them with myrrh." she continued, "and brush them carefully over your skin. It will make your face look like translucent marble."

The girl who had been working on the hair now finished and stepped around to look at Zebidah's face. "Wow! You're gorgeous. The king's heart will beat faster when he sees you."

"You think so?"

"Positively."

"Oh, I hope so. I do so want him to love me." The room became silent. It was the first time anyone had mentioned "love." In all the arrangements that had been made between families, nothing had ever been said about it. Marriage was how families shared their wealth and produced the next generation. "I-I-I hope he loves me," she whispered.

Greatly sobered at the thought, one of her servants slowly spoke to the future queen of Judah. "If you treat him kindly, and do whatever you can to make him happy . . . don't you think that you can make him love you? that love will come in its time?"

"I hope so."

Quietly the girls dressed Zebidah and finished arranging her hair. Decked with many jewels, she wore a thin gold bejeweled crown. Her earrings, nose ring, strands of pearls, a dozen bracelets on each wrist, finger rings, anklets, and toe rings gave her the effect of stars twinkling brightly in the night sky.

Before she ever left the nobleman's home, she looked every bit a queen.

Josiah's preparations, though different, were just as time-consuming, and done with as much care as that of the bride.

"Why don't I entwine garlands of fresh flowers about his golden crown," one of the men servants suggested.

"That would look lovely," replied Jedidah. Turning to her son's personal servant, she said, "And why don't we scent his clothing with frankincense and myrrh. That will mask any unpleasant odors."

"It'll be cool outside," Josiah objected. "Why would I sweat?"

"Oh, you will," another servant smiled.

"I'm going to add a sash around his waist," the personal servant stated. Not expecting an answer, he was merely commenting on what he was doing.

"These sandals are really beautiful." The queen mother held them up for all to see. "This is the first time I've seen a groom wear special sandals like this."

"He is king," the personal servant replied solemnly. "He must have special sandals."

When Josiah had finished dressing, his robes flowed gracefully to his feet, and his hair and peach-fuzz beard had been combed to perfection.

"He's one handsome young man," one of the servants remarked to Jedidah.

The queen mother felt a pride within her heart that threatened to burst her chest.

The king's entourage gathered in the palace garden. The air sparkled with laughter and joking—the joyful anticipation that their king would soon wed. "I can't wait to see her," a groomsman laughed. "I hope she's pretty."

"Shaphan told me that she is beautiful," Josiah replied, unable to hide his excitement. "He said she was beautiful, intelligent, and witty."

The royal party soon wormed its way out the palace gate and down the street. Since the streets of Jerusalem did not have any illumination, each man carried a lamp or a torch to light the way. At the house where the bride stayed, a herald soon announced in a loud voice: "The king is coming! The king is coming!"

The bride appeared at the door, followed by her maidservants. When the royal party arrived, Josiah offered his hand to her, and Zebidah took hold of it, and joined the procession back to the palace, her servants close behind. Relatives of the bride went ahead of the wedding train to scatter ears of parched grain to the children along the way. Some of the men had brought along their musical instruments and drums, and their songs and shouts of joy filled the city.

A musician sang a psalm of David:

"In embroidered garments she is led to the king;
    her virgin companions follow her
    and are brought to you.
They are led in with joy and gladness;
    they enter the palace of the king.
Your sons will take the place of your fathers;
    you will make them princes throughout
    the land."[3]

Jedidah watched from one of the palace windows as the procession neared the garden. "My heart is filled to overflowing," she confessed to her personal servant.

"I know," the older woman said. "I remember when my son brought home his bride. It's a wonderful time. And now the king takes a bride. Yahweh will bless him with many sons."

"Yes," the queen mother agreed. "With many sons."

By this time the procession had flowed through the garden and into the palace throne room that would serve as the grand banquet hall.

"May Yahweh bless this house!" an official proclaimed. "The king brings home his bride!"

"Amen!" everyone chorused.

Shouts of joy rang out when Zebidah crossed the threshold of the palace. It had now become her home.

She and Josiah stood side by side on the raised platform before the throne, both filled with a mixture of excitement, anticipation, and nervousness. Each wondered about the days ahead as they would learn to love each other. Shaphan, raising his hands over them, pronounced a benediction.

The wedding feast would go on for seven more days. But this was the moment they remembered the most.

---

[1] Later known as the Sea of Galilee.

[2] Kohl was an eye shadow cosmetic made from galena (a gray lead ore) mixed with gum and water.

[3] Psalm 45:14–16, NIV.

Chapter 6

Winning the First Round

"You're so kind," Zebidah remarked one morning as they talked together. "None of the men in Rumah treat their wives is well as you do me."

"I love you," Josiah assured her. "But even if I hadn't learned to love you, I would treat you kindly, for that is Yahweh's way." He tickled the feet of his newborn son, Eliakim, and smiled at the child's giggling and cooing.

"I have noticed that you go to the Temple twice a day to pray to this Yahweh. And you mention Him often. Many of the people in our village worship Baal, but they don't speak of him as you do of Yahweh. Why is that?"

"Baal may be their god, but he isn't kind and good, as Yahweh is. People do not love him, but rather fear him. They believe that if they do not sacrifice to him, he will be angry with them and withhold the rain, or ruin their crops, or some other bad thing."

"But Yahweh is not like that, is He?" She picked up their son and began to change his loincloths.

The king took a drink of water from the goblet he'd taken from a table next to his chair, and smacked his lips before he continued. "No. Yahweh sends the rain on the good and the bad just as He sends the sunshine on the good and the bad." Josiah stopped and gazed at his wife and then at his son. "He loves everyone. You see, He is the God who created the world and everything in it, including you and me . . . and Eliakim."

"Really?"

"Yes. And since He made us, He blesses us and wants us to be happy and to love each other."

"And that's why you are so kind to me?"

"Yahweh loves you. And so do I."

"And what about your other wife, Hamutal? Does God love her, too?"

"Yes, God loves Hamutal, and the baby she will soon bear. I hope you and Hamutal will learn to love each other. It would make me very happy to have a loving household.

"It's very difficult, of course." Zebidah frowned as she lay Eliakim in his cradle. "I love you so much, but it's hard to think of sharing you with someone else." She bit her lip. "I cried for a week when you married her." Tears glistened in the corners of her eyes. "I tried to keep it from you."

"You didn't." Josiah spoke in a soft voice, staring out through the window opening in the wall at the gardens and the roofs of the houses beyond. The music of flutes and frame drums came from the street below, as well as the shouts of children as they danced to the tunes. "I would not have chosen to marry Hamutal. But the council, and Mother, both said it was necessary for a king to have several wives. 'He must have many sons so that he will have an heir to the throne,'" he mimicked the voice of the prime minister.

Zebidah laughed in spite of herself. "I know. All kings are expected to have many wives. Will you have to marry any others?"

"I hope not!"

The two of them laughed together, and reached out to touch hands.

At 20, Josiah had reigned 12 years, and God had richly blessed him. Many of the people now followed his lead in worshipping Yahweh at the morning and evening services. It had begun to be difficult to find a place to stand.

"Something must be done about the Temple," Josiah stated to Hilkiah, the high priest, as they sat in the priest's chamber. "There are so many idols and other trappings lying around that there is not enough room for the worshippers."

"That is true. What do you suggest we do? I don't know if I have the authority to do it myself."

"You *do* have the authority," Josiah chided in a gentle way. "But I will help you."

"How can you do that?"

"I think the first thing we need to do is round up the priests of other gods and the male and female prostitutes who live in the Temple rooms, and then get rid of their idols and shrines. The ancient law of Yahweh requires that leaders of idolatry be executed for their sins." The king looked past Hilkiah at the frost still covering the plants in the Temple garden. "Then we'll have to raise some money for repairs."

"In the name of the king, you are under arrest!" Hilkiah declared as Josiah stood beside him. A sizable group of soldiers formed a U formation around them.

"Why?" shouted a worshipper at one of the pagan altars in the Temple courtyard. "King Manasseh set up this shrine and gave us his permis . . ."

"I'm revoking Manasseh's ruling." Josiah held his scepter across his chest. "You must obey the high priest. You are all under arrest—both you and the male and female prostitutes who practice their trade in the Temple chambers."

"Give us mercy," the pagan priests began to plead, falling onto their faces before Josiah. "We'll take our sacred articles and leave if you will . . ."

"I can show you no mercy," Josiah interrupted. "You have broken the sacred law of Yahweh, and under that law you must be punished."

The priests' faces blanched, for they knew the law. "Have pity on us," cried the main priest of the shrine. "We will worship Yahweh. We . . ."

"Enough," the king shouted. "Captain"—he turned to the soldiers who stood at attention—"take these men captive. Send a platoon through the Temple chambers and arrest all the male and female prostitutes. Bring them here before me."

"Yes, Your Majesty." The officer bowed to Josiah, and gave orders to his men. Soon they fanned out across the Temple courts to carry out their duties. Within minutes the soldiers had rounded up more than 15 male and female cult prostitutes, ordering them to fall on the ground before their monarch. The guards then bound their hands behind their backs.

"Captain?"

"Yes, sir."

"The sacred law of Yahweh requires that all who lead God's people into the worship of pagan deities should be executed. Take these people to the Valley of Hinnom and behead them. Then cast their bodies in the place where dead animals are tossed."

"No! No!" the pagan priests protested. "Please! Have mercy on us! We promise to serve Yahweh! Please, don't kill us!"

But the soldiers jerked them to their feet and led them, kicking and screaming, to the place of execution. Josiah followed to assure that his orders were carried out. A crowd of people gathered to see the grizzly sight.

Afterward the king led his armed guard back into the city. The soldiers returned to their barracks and Josiah to his palace. As he entered his chambers he burst into deep retching sobs that shook his whole body. He sank onto a chair near the entrance, totally drained. "O Yahweh!" he exclaimed, lifting his hands and face upward, "I know that You require the executions that we did today. But Lord, my heart goes out to those people. My soul cannot stomach what I have seen. Please help me. Give me strength for times like these."

Jedidah happened into the hall just at that moment. "What is the matter, Josiah?" she asked as she hurried toward him. "Whatever would cause you such grief?"

Her son sketched the events of the past few hours. By this time Zebidah and Hamutal had joined them.

"Was it really necessary to execute all those people?" Zebidah questioned. "There are priests and priestesses all over the country. Will we have to kill them all?"

"I'm afraid so," Josiah explained between sobs. "Yahweh cannot allow anything that will draw people away from worshipping Him, for He is our Creator. He is the only one who deserves our worship."

Jedidah looked down at the floor for a minute. "I've served Yahweh faithfully all my life," she mused aloud. "And I never knew this side of Him. I never knew that it was a life-or-death matter." Then she looked thoughtful. "But I'm beginning to realize why," she continued a moment later. "If we allow anyone to draw Yahweh's children away to the worship of pagan gods, it could destroy the whole nation."

"That's true," Zebidah added. "When I compare the worship of Yahweh to what we called the 'worship' of the local gods, I see that Yahweh is kind and loving, even though He destroys those who fight against Him." Sadly she smiled at her husband. "I'm sure that it was not easy to see all those people executed today. But think of the twisted lives they lived and the evils they led other people to do. Even your own father fell for their lies.

"Perhaps people will stop thinking of the Temple as a place to worship just any god. Perhaps they will once more regard it as the house of Yahweh."

Jedidah felt tears run down her cheek. *If Manasseh, in his final years, had taken the steps that his grandson is now doing, my husband would probably still be alive.* But she forced a smile, for she admired her son's courage.

~

"Well, the pagan cults are gone." Hilkiah told King Josiah before the morning sacrifice. "But most of their trappings still litter the Temple. We have a lot of work to do cleaning up after them."

"I know. But we've won the first round. Someday we'll destroy idolatry completely."

"We need to repair much of the Temple structure," the high priest observed. "You see, there, how the steps have worn away, and how blocks are missing from the inner wall of the court. My men tell me that one of the foundation stones has split and needs replacing. Some of the areas on the outer wall have begun to crumble."

"We need to repair it all," the king replied. "Are there other things that need to be done?"

"Yes. The rooms that the cult prostitutes occupied need to be completely renovated so that they can be rededicated for the use of visiting priests from the surrounding cities." Hilkiah stopped for a moment. "Then there's the chamber that Ahaz, father of Hezekiah, had built on top of the priests' quarters, the one from which he worshipped the stars."

"Tear it down," Josiah commanded.

"I thought you'd feel that way. But it will require some doing, because it's more difficult to take down something constructed of stone at that height than it is to build it. We must make sure that each stone is lowered carefully, or someone might be injured or killed.

"There are also rooms that the pagan priests took over, that should be used for the treasury and the scribes. These will need to be cleansed and repaired so that they can again be employed for their intended purpose. And . . ."

"I can see that the work is great, and it will need a large amount of money for hiring laborers and purchasing materials." Josiah scanned the hills outside Jerusalem. "I believe that those quarries that produced limestone for the first building are still in use. You can probably get whatever stone you need from there, and I believe the copper mines in the desert in the south can supply you with material for the tools you will need."

The king put his finger to his lips. "It might be a good idea to place boxes near the Temple gates so that people will be able to drop in offerings for the repair work. What do you think?"

"It worked for King Joash," Hilkiah nodded. "He collected enough to do all the repairs required in his day. Yes . . . we'll do that.

"I noticed Queen Zebidah worshipping among the women this morning," Hilkiah said, changing the subject.

"She told me of her decision last night." A delighted smile showed his joy. "During the past few months she has asked many questions. The final thing that helped her to decide happened to be the executions yesterday."

"Really?"

"Yes. She saw Yahweh in a much different light when she compared Him to the gods she used to worship. 'Only a God of love,' she said, 'would protect His people even at the loss of His wicked children who lead them astray.' The queen realizes that Yahweh, unlike the other gods, cares whether people worship Him or not. That He is a God of all people, not just the rulers of Judah. It pleases me greatly that she has decided to turn to Yahweh as her God."

"Her presence will go far in convincing many of the women to come back to God."

"I pray that you're right."

The priest turned and assumed his position for the morning sacrifice. And Josiah took his place for worship.

"Captain." The head of the guard stood at attention before Josiah. "I want you to take your men throughout Judah and destroy all the pagan shrines and high places and execute all those directly connected with its operation—priests, cult prostitutes . . . Employ as many men as you think necessary. You will have to move with haste, for we don't want people fleeing from justice when they hear news of the purge in Jerusalem."

"Yes, sir." The officer started to leave the throne room, then paused near the entrance. "What shall I do if any of our soldiers refuses to take part in the purge?" he said, again facing the king.

"Just replace him."

"Yes, sir." With that he left.

"Excuse me, Your Majesty." Judah's chief general strode into the palace courtroom.

Josiah turned from a discussion with the governor of Jerusalem about the removal of waste from the city streets.

"I'm sorry to interrupt your conference, but I have news of great importance."

"It's all right." Josiah showed a slight annoyance, but it passed as soon as it came. "We're finished anyway." He motioned for the city official to leave.

"Your Majesty"—the general seemed out of breath—"my scouts tell me that the Assyrians are on the move."

"Do you have any idea of their intended target?"

"That's the strange thing. There doesn't seem to be any

target. They are leaving all the fortress cities and moving northward along the King's Highway. While they have guards covering their flanks, they don't seem to be prepared for battle." He scratched his cheek through his beard. "They act as though they're in a hurry, but don't seem to be ready for war."

"That is strange," Josiah agreed. "Keep me posted. We don't want to be caught off guard."

Soon after the general's report, a member of the royal messenger corps stood at the entrance of the court, waiting to be acknowledged.

Josiah beckoned for the messenger. "What news do you bring?"

"Your Majesty." The messenger bowed at the waist briefly when he reached the throne. "I have news that seems to be of importance." He paused, looking directly into the king's eyes. "The Assyrians seem to be withdrawing their troops from all the provinces, and summoning them to Nineveh. There seems to be a threat to their homeland, and they need all their forces at home."

"Do you know what the danger might be?"

"Not for sure, though it may be Babylon. Reports have reached us that it has revolted against Assyria."

"Perhaps that's it." The king thought a moment. "Keep me informed."

Assyria had caused great suffering for Judah during the reigns of Hezekiah and Manasseh. They had overwhelmed Israel to the north, and carried the entire nation into exile. Yet they hadn't rattled their swords a great deal of late. But to abandon conquered territory entirely? It didn't make international or political sense.

I wonder what they're up to, Josiah thought as he mulled over the news. *Could it be that they are in real trouble themselves? That would be wonderful! We would then be free to follow our own plans. And best of all, we wouldn't have to pay huge taxes to them anymore!*

The Temple Gates

News of international politics and wars arrived at the palace on a daily basis. "It seems that our great nemesis has given up his control of this area," Josiah confided to Zebidah one night as they lay in bed.

"That's wonderful," she said, her head on his shoulder. "They gave us no end of trouble in Rumah when I was a girl. Raiding us every year or so, they killed many people and carried many into captivity. We were always terrified!" She stopped for a moment, and when she spoke again, her voice quivered. "They took my uncle to Nineveh, and he became a slave to some nobleman. He was a nobleman in Rumah, a member of the council of elders."

"I'm so sorry," he said as she buried her face against his chest. "But now the Assyrians are gone. We at least can be thankful for that."

"Yes," She wiped her tears with a corner of the bed covering.

When she drifted off into sleep, he soon followed.

Chapter 7

The Beginning
of Reformation

"Executing those in charge of the cult shrines in the Temple is just a beginning, you know." Hilkiah met his king after the evening services as both left the Temple through the Royal Gate—the gate leading from the Temple court into the palace grounds.

"I know." Josiah turned and scrutinized the Asherah pole on the Mount of Olives. The pole stood taller than any other in the area. For some reason, the soldiers had bypassed it in their haste to get to all the sites before news of the purge could reach them. The royal guard feared that tidings of the fate of the priests in the shrine there would cause the guilty priests at other high places to flee as well. They wanted to round them all up so they could put an end to idolatry in Judah.

Because the soldiers had ignored the high place on the Mount of Olives, the priests and prostitutes there decided they were safe from the royal edict.

"I will destroy that shrine myself," Josiah announced as he talked with the high priest. "Assign some of your priests and Levites to continue the work on the Temple." The king glanced around at the work to be done. "Have your men hire additional laborers to begin the repairs."

Marching at the head of the palace guard, the young

monarch ascended the road up the mountain ridge that stood east of Jerusalem. As they neared the top, Josiah saw pagan priests and others fleeing in several directions. "Get them," he commanded, and guards pursued the fugitives. Within minutes the soldiers returned, prodding their captives before them.

"Do you have all of them?" the king asked.

"I believe we have," the officer in charge replied.

"Execute them as we did those in the Temple."

The priests and cult prostitutes struggled to free themselves from their captors, but it was no use. Each met his or her fate under the swing of the executioner's sword.

As king, Josiah had to observe the slaughter in order to make sure his orders were carried out. Some of the soldiers carried the bodies to the center of the shrine. The corpses would defile the pagan shrine. Other soldiers went to work destroying the cult objects they found in the area. Pulling down the Asherah pole, they chopped it into firewood, and built a large fire on the place where the altar had stood. The corpses of those who had desecrated the spot they now tossed onto the fire. When the flames died away, only bones and skulls remained. These were scattered around the shrine. The presence of human bones defiled the entire area, and made it unusable for any religious purpose.

As the men finished, the sun sank behind the city walls of Jerusalem. "You've done your work well." Josiah told his guards. "You've rid the area of the evil that has been drawing God's people away from Him. I realize that it's been unpleasant work, but it was absolutely necessary. I adjure all you, by the living God, to learn to love Yahweh and worship Him alone."

As Josiah surveyed his grim-faced men, he realized that they would be confused at how they could love a God who demanded such seeming cruelty. "God loves His people with an undying love," the king explained. "He grieves that these people have gone astray and have paid for their crimes by the shedding of their blood. But think of all the people that they have led into lives of sin; all the men whose relationships with their wives and families have been ruined by these pagan prostitutes; all the sons of God who have become sons of the evil one because they have forsaken Yahweh to worship sticks and stones. God loves His people too much to let this kind of iniquity continue." He paused to catch his breath. "And you have been God's hands to purify His land, so His people can be safe to serve Him."

The men stood in silence for several minutes. Finally one of the soldiers in the rear shouted "Amen." Faltering at first, then with growing conviction, the others chorused, "Amen!"

His shoulders slumped, tears trickling down his cheeks, Josiah returned to his chambers in the palace. Again he mourned. Even though the people at the shrine had been evil and the law of God had condemned them to be put death, he still felt drained from what had happened on the Mount of Olives.

"I know you are exhausted, Your Majesty." The prime minister approached from the direction of the council room. "But news has come from Assyria that you should know."

Josiah shoved the events of the day into another chamber of his mind. "Yes, let me hear the news."

The prime minister led him into the council room. Servants had placed a table in front of the small throne and lit several lamps so the men could see the documents spread out on its surface.

"Here are messages from the royal scouts." The general and the counselors gathered around the table, while the military officer explained the reports to him. "Assyria has reached its day of reckoning. The Babylonians and others have rebelled and have broken away from Assyrian domination."

The general pointed to a rough charcoal sketch on a

piece of limestone. "Here is Assyria," he pointed to a region outlined on the diagram. "Their capital city, Nineveh, lies about 800 miles north of us. Over here, southeast of Nineveh, is the great city of Babylon. It has been the pride of the Assyrian Empire. To lose this city would greatly weaken them. But Babylon has revolted, and the Assyrians have called in their army from all the empire to fight against Babylon in order to retake the territory."

"That explains the reports of whole Assyrian armies moving north," Josiah commented. "They're going to save the most important part of their empire."

"What happens to us now that the Assyrians are gone?" the prime minister asked.

"I guess we're free to do what we want," the commanding general commented.

The news seemed too good to be true. Josiah's head seemed to swim. After the gruesome events of the day, the political news brought a sense of relief. In effect, the withdrawal of Assyria left Judah free to follow its own path—and to press the spiritual reform to the area of the old northern kingdom, as well.

The armies of Assyria and Babylon clashed on the plains at Sallat, just northwest of Sippar, near the Euphrates River. Thousands fell on both sides. As the day wore on, the center of the Assyrian line began to crumble as the Babylonians pushed them hard, slaughtering their enemy mercilessly. The ends of the Assyrian ranks saw that part of their army had begun to fall back, and they began to retreat as well. Soon, little by little, Assyrian platoons began to flee in ever growing numbers. The Assyrian officers shouted at their men to turn and fight, but to no avail. It seemed now that no one could stop the Babylonians.

The Beginning of Reformation

Assyria had lost the province and city of Babylon, as well as thousands of its finest warriors. Nineveh had received partial payment for the terror it had spread to all the nations, from Asia to Africa. But more punishment was yet to come.

The retreat became a rout, and the way to Nineveh was carpeted with Assyrian bodies. The Babylonian hosts pressed the day, and were it not for the setting sun, they might have slaughtered the entire Assyrian army. But the weary, defeated troops of Nineveh pushed on through the night, helping the wounded who had escaped, leaving behind those who lay on the battlefields to die during the night or in the hot sun of the coming day.

Jedidah, Zebidah, and Hamutal sat with Josiah in his bedchamber as he reclined on the bed. "You have done a brave thing," the king's mother said. "And it needed to be done. I'm also pleased with the report that your soldiers have successfully eliminated so many of the other pagan shrines of Judah."

"It's a grizzly task," Zebidah added. "But Yahweh's name must be guarded."

"Besides all that," Josiah commented, raising himself on one arm, "the Assyrians have relinquished control of this area. For the first time in 100 years we are *free*." With a faraway look in his eyes he continued: "Perhaps I can bring back the northern tribes into one dominion again." He glanced, first at his mother, and then at his wives. "God has given us the opportunity to bring *all* Israel back to Him."

"When will you begin?" the queen mother asked.

"Tomorrow," the weary man answered. "In the meantime I must get some rest." With that, his eyes closed, and he fell asleep so quickly that the women glanced at each other in surprise.

Chapter 8

The Scroll

"You're right," Shaphan said as he took the roll of papyrus from Hilkiah, broke the seal, and opened the covering. "This scroll must be of great importance. Where did you find it?"

"Some workmen discovered it while cleaning out an abandoned storage room. I think it's a book of the Law," Hilkiah breathed. "We must handle it with the utmost of care."

Shaphan took the scroll, laid it on his table, and slowly rolled it open. The material was old and stiff. "I'll have to spend some time examining this. I'll report to you later."

The more the scribe pored over it, the more alarmed he became. "Ahhh!" he moaned. "We stand condemned before God!" Hurriedly he rerolled the scroll, replaced it in its covering, spoke briefly with the high priest, and together they hurried off to the palace.

"Your Majesty." They caught their breath after rushing from the Temple.

Josiah strolled toward them from the royal quarters. "What is it?"

"The workmen have found a book of the Law in the Temple," Shaphan blurted out. "It's terrible, my king. We're doomed!"

"Calm down, Shaphan!" The king smiled to see one of his chief officers in such a state. But he realized that it must be something of life-or-death importance, and an expression of deep concern soon replaced the smile.

"Your Majesty," the scribe began again. He now spoke

more calmly as the high priest stood quietly behind him. "Some of the workmen cleaning out an old forgotten storage room found this scroll of the Law in an old jar. I've read it, Your Majesty, and it contains divine curses against the idolatry that has so prevailed among the people. If I interpret it correctly, the curses extend to us and to all future generations."

The three of them retired to the council chamber, where Shaphan rolled the scroll out on the table. He read some of the passages to the king.

"Cursed is the man who carves an image or casts an idol— a thing detestable to the Lord, the work of the craftsman's hands—and sets it up in secret. If you do not obey the Lord your God and do not carefully follow all his commands and decrees I am giving you today, all these curses will come upon you and overtake you: You will be cursed in the city and cursed in the country. Your basket and your kneading trough will be cursed. The fruit of your womb will be cursed, and the crops of your land, and the calves of your herds and the lambs of your flocks. You will be cursed when you come in and cursed when you go out. The Lord will send on you curses, confusion and rebuke in everything you put your hand to, until you are destroyed and come to sudden ruin because of the evil you have done in forsaking him. . . . The Lord will cause you to be defeated before your enemies. You will come at them from one direction but flee from them in seven, and you will become a thing of horror to all the kingdoms on earth. Your carcasses will be food for all the birds of the air and the beasts of the earth, and there will be no one to frighten them away. . . . Your sons and daughters will be given to another nation, and you will wear out your eyes watching for them day after day, powerless to lift a hand. A people that you do not know will eat what your land and labor produce, and you will have nothing but cruel oppression all your days. . . . The Lord will drive you and the king you set over you to a nation unknown to you or your fathers. There you will worship other gods, gods of wood and stone. You will become a thing of horror and an object of scorn and ridicule to all the nations where the Lord will drive you. . . . You will have sons and daughters but you will not keep them, because they will go into captivity. . . . All these curses will come upon you. They will pursue you and overtake you until you are destroyed, because you did not obey the Lord your God and observe the commands and decrees he gave you. They will be a sign and a wonder to you and your descendants forever. Because you did not serve the Lord your God joyfully and gladly in the time of prosperity, therefore in hunger and thirst, in nakedness and dire poverty, you will serve the enemies the Lord sends against you. He will put an iron yoke on your neck until he has destroyed you. The Lord will bring a nation against you from far away, from the ends of the earth, like an eagle swooping down, a nation whose language you will not understand, a fierce-looking nation without respect for the old or pity for the young. . . . They will lay siege to all the cities throughout your land until the high fortified walls in which you trust fall down. They will besiege all the cities throughout the land the Lord your God is giving you. Because of the suffering that your enemy will inflict on you during the siege, you will eat the fruit of the womb, the flesh of the sons and daughters the Lord your God has given you. . . . If you do not carefully follow all the words of this law, which are written in this book, and do not revere this glorious and awesome name—the Lord your God—the Lord will send fearful plagues on you and your descendants, harsh and prolonged disasters, and severe and lingering illnesses. . . . The Lord will also bring on you every kind of sickness and disaster not recorded in this Book of the Law, until you are destroyed. You who were as numerous as the stars in the sky will be left but few in number, because you did not obey the Lord your God. . . . Then the Lord will scatter you among all nations, from one end of the earth to the other.

The Scroll

There you will worship other gods—gods of wood and stone, which neither you nor your fathers have known. Among those nations you will find no repose, no resting place for the sole of your foot. There the Lord will give you an anxious mind, eyes weary with longing, and a despairing heart. You will live in constant suspense, filled with dread both night and day, never sure of your life."[1]

By the time he had finished, he had gone through much of the scroll.

"That's terrible," the king gasped. "Great is Yahweh's anger! I'm sure it will be poured out on us just as it says in that book." The king began to pace about the room. "Our fathers have not kept the word of the Lord." Josiah tore his royal robes to show his grief. "They have not done what was written in this book."[2]

Josiah did not say anything for a moment, weighing the matter in His mind. "Does the curse still strike us if we have repented? We must know!" He continued to pace. "Perhaps we should seek counsel from one of Yahweh's prophets. Whom should we go to? Jeremiah? Zephaniah? Huldah? Habakkuk?"

"I believe that Huldah would be best able to bring us the word of the Lord at this time." Shaphan seemed confident of his decision.

"Then have several of the elders and counselors accompany you. Take the scroll and ask Huldah what we should do. May God go with you."

Shaphan, Hilkiah the high priest, Ahikam (Shaphan's son), Achbor, and Asaiah, the king's servant, slowly made the trek to the Second Quarter, where Huldah lived. They had put on sackcloth and had sprinkled ashes on their heads. Many along the way wondered at the mourning of the kingdom's highest leaders. When the men knocked at her door,

Huldah rose to welcome them into her home. She already knew they were coming, their identities, and their mission. It was not even necessary to open the scroll. The Lord had revealed to her the answer she should give them.

"God's wrath has been kindled like a fire that cannot be quenched," she told them. "Once kindled, that fire will burn until the nation has been consumed." She paused to allow them to grasp the importance of her message. "Even though Josiah has sought to make reforms, the nation is guilty, and the reforms cannot save it."

"But—" She stopped them as they solemnly rose to leave. "Tell the king of Judah, . . . 'This is what the Lord, the God of Israel, says concerning the words you heard: Because your heart was responsive and you humbled yourself before God when you heard what he spoke against this place and its people, and because you humbled yourself before me and tore your robes and wept in my presence, I have heard you, declares the Lord. Now I will gather you to your fathers, and you will be buried in peace. Your eyes will not see the disaster I am going to bring on this place and on those who live here.' "[3]

The heavyhearted counselors, when they returned to the palace, found Josiah sitting on the platform below the throne. Concerned that their report would be a blow to the king, they prayed that he would not abandon his reforms.

"I was afraid of that," Josiah admitted when the men presented Huldah's message. Obtaining some ashes from a brazier used to heat the room, he sprinkled them on his head. "Whatever we do to restore the faithfulness of the people, it will all come to nothing. Judah will be lost."

Just then the king noticed a movement out of the corner of his eye and glanced toward the doorway. He recognized immediately the young man advancing toward him. Jeremiah, near the age of Josiah, walked so closely with God that Josiah actually envied him, wishing such an experience for himself.

"Your Majesty." The counselors turned at the sound of the young prophet's voice.

"Jeremiah." Josiah smiled faintly.

"I grieve, as you do," the seer continued, "for the idolatry that plagues our nation. But I have been gratified to witness the work of reform that you have done. Yahweh is indeed pleased with your work." Jeremiah smiled, and nodded to the others standing near the throne. "Do not think that your work is useless. It is not. Even though the nation will perish because of its sins, think of all the people whose lives your work will have touched. Your efforts at reform will impress many of the people in your kingdom, and they will decide to be faithful to Yahweh—just because you, King Josiah, love God and serve Him faithfully."

"Thank you, Jeremiah." The king hung his head for a moment. "I was at the point of quitting. But you have opened my eyes to a greater vision. As long as God gives me breath, I will fight evil and encourage good."

"My people." King Josiah looked over the hundreds who had come to the Temple as a result of his invitation. "You know of my zeal to purge the country of idolatry. I mean to continue until the only God worshipped in all of Judah will be Yahweh, Creator of heaven and earth." He paused and searched their faces to see their response to what he had said.

"Some of you, I'm sure, have been upset by deaths of those belonging to the shrines I have ordered destroyed. It has upset me as well." For a second he swallowed hard, stared at the ground, then once more faced the crowd. "The news of our actions has spread all over the country, and every priest and prostitute in the kingdom knew what would happen to them if they remained unrepentant, the reason for the judgment, and how they could save their lives." Another pause. "They needed only to have repented of their ways and brought their sin offerings to the Temple, and God would have forgiven them.

"Even now," he continued, "there are many shrines, with pagan high places, that are still open in the kingdom. All of those priests and attendants know how they can save their lives—by coming back to God. Anyone executed because of their leadership of pagan worship dies only because he or she has refused the grace of God.

"Today I want to show you why I'm so zealous for Yahweh. Recently a book of the Law of God has been found in the Temple, and the book explains it all." Then he gestured toward the Temple scribe. "Shaphan, will you read the scroll for us?"

The scribe read in the high-pitched, monotone voice he had learned in scribal school. It took more than an hour, and some of the children became restless. As a result, their mothers missed some of the details. But all realized the gravity of the message presented to them.

By the time Shaphan had finished reading, many wept softly, while others mourned loudly. Everyone realized how far they had come from the plan that God had laid out for them, and had written in His book. It spelled out the blessings that would come to those who served God faithfully. But it had also explained the curses that would strike the nation if the people went astray. There lingered no question in any mind that Yahweh loved them with an everlasting love—that, in fact, He did not want any of them to die, that all should come to repentance.

But it was just as plain that Yahweh would not allow any of His people to follow false gods and to lead others to do so. He knew how much His children would suffer by adopting such a foolish course, and He had to remove the rebels in order to save those who would be led astray by their example. And the entire nation had gone so . . . so far, in fact, that they realized that the curses would surely fall upon them and their children.

"Have we gone too far?" asked one man in the group.

"Yes," answered their sad-faced king. "But all God's threatenings are conditional.[4] If we come back to God and sincerely worship Him; if we rid the kingdom of all the high places and pagan shrines, it may be that God will repent of the evil that He has said He will do." He glanced briefly at the pavement as he began to weep. When he had again gained control of himself, he looked back at the assembly. "My dear people"—tears trickled down his cheeks—"repent of your sins, leave behind your evil ways, and bring your offerings to the Temple. God will forgive you. It may be that the threatened curses will delay, or that perhaps they will not fall at all."

Josiah stood near Boaz, the great bronze pillar beside which he had been anointed king. "What shall we do? Shall we continue as we have been, and let the disaster come? Or shall we renew the covenant with God, cast out our idols, and bring our sin offerings to Yahweh?"

Every voice shouted at once, as though it had been choreographed by the Temple choir director: "Renew the covenant! Renew the covenant!"

The king's heart leaped for joy as he smiled broadly and his tears turned to those of rejoicing. "Hilkiah"—he turned to the high priest—"renew the covenant with the people."

Hardly able to believe his ears, the high priest at first had difficulty speaking. Then, at last, he found his voice. "The covenant is in the Ten Commandments that God gave our fathers at Mount Sinai. Read them for us, Shaphan."

The scribe rolled the parchment of another scroll until he had found the place.

"I am the Lord your God, who brought you out of Egypt, out of the land of slavery. You shall have no other gods before me.

"You shall not make for yourself an idol in the form of anything in heaven above or on the earth beneath or in the waters below. You shall not bow down to them or worship them; for I, the Lord your God, am a jealous God, punishing the children for [partaking in] the sin of the fathers to the third and fourth generation of those who hate me, but showing love to a thousand generations of those who love me and keep my commandments.

"You shall not misuse the name of the Lord your God, for the Lord will not hold anyone guiltless who misuses his name.

"Observe the Sabbath day by keeping it holy, as the Lord your God has commanded you. Six days you shall labor and do all your work, but the seventh day is a Sabbath to the Lord your God. On it you shall not do any work, neither you, nor your son or daughter, nor your manservant or maidservant, nor your ox, your donkey or any of your animals, nor the alien within your gates, so that your manservant and maidservant may rest, as you do. Remember that you were slaves in Egypt and that the Lord your God brought you out of there with a mighty hand and an outstretched arm. Therefore the Lord your God has commanded you to observe the Sabbath day.

"Honor your father and your mother, as the Lord your God has commanded you, so that you may live long and that it may go well with you in the land the Lord your God is giving you.

"You shall not murder.

"You shall not commit adultery.

"You shall not steal.

"You shall not give false testimony against your neighbor.

"You shall not covet your neighbor's wife. You shall not set your desire on your neighbor's house or land, his manservant or maidservant, his ox or donkey, or anything that belongs to your neighbor."[5]

"This is the covenant that Yahweh our God made with

us at Sinai."[6] Hilkiah extended his hands upward, in the form of a V. "Because we cannot keep them on our own, we must permit Yahweh's Spirit to keep these commandments through us." He paused, and then continued: "People! Will you make this covenant with God today?"

The resounding "Amen!" must have been heard across the valley, even to the Mount of Olives.

"Then let it be known this day that God's Spirit will keep this covenant through you as long as you allow Him to live in your hearts. Now, bring your sin offerings as the law commands."

Several pagan priests and cult prostitutes stood in the crowd that day. Many of them felt the conviction that the Spirit brought upon their hearts. Repentant, they too brought their sin offerings to God.

But some spurned the covenant and those who made it. "We will not serve Yahweh, nor will we make a covenant with Him," they sneered. "Go on, if you must. But leave us out."

Many thousands of people made their covenant with Yahweh on that day, and Josiah praised God for the marvelous miracle He had worked in Judah. "Blessed be God, my Savior," he sang as he returned to his home that day.

Jedidah and Josiah's wives had been in the Temple and, with the others, renewed the covenant with God. Now they stood on the threshold and threw their arms around their king: "God has blessed us all today," they sang together as they became enmeshed in each other's arms.

---

[1] Deuteronomy 27:15-28:66, NIV.
[2] See 2 Chronicles 34:21.
[3] Verses 26–28, NIV.
[4] Compare Ezekiel 18:21, 22, et al.
[5] Deuteronomy 5:6-21, NIV.
[6] See Exodus 34:28.

Chapter 9

Passover

"Your Majesty." Zephaniah the prophet stood before the king.

"Zephaniah, to what do I owe this privilege?"

"Yahweh honors what you've done by destroying the idolatrous shrines, and the people who served in them." The prophet smiled. "He is also pleased by the progress in the repair and cleansing of the Temple, and most of all by your leading the people in the renewing of their covenant with Him."

"Thank You, Yahweh." Josiah looked toward heaven. "I have had no other thought in mind than to bring glory to Your name."

"God understands your motives and is blessing you for your faithfulness." The prophet shifted his feet and folded his arms. "However, Yahweh wants for you to lead the people in the Passover and the Feast of Unleavened Bread."

"That's right." Josiah thought a moment. "We are approaching the time of the Passover."

"Yes."

"And you say that God wants me to take charge in this?"

"Yes. You will, of course, lead through encouraging the people, and the priests will do their part in the Temple rites."

"If I remember correctly, from hearing the Law of Moses"—Josiah shifted his position on his throne—"the Passover feast itself takes place in the homes of the people."

"Then on the following morning—the Sabbath of the

Feast of Unleavened Bread—special offerings will be burned in the Temple."

"All right," the king nodded. "I'll see that the preparation begins immediately."

"God bless you, my lord."

The chief priests sat with Josiah in the council room, their chairs arranged in a semicircle. Among them were elders of families of Anothoth, the town from which Jeremiah came, along with Hilkiah, Shaphan, and Ahikam, son of Shaphan. Hilkiah was the first to speak.

"If I understand you, sir, you believe that we should celebrate the Passover on the fourteenth of Nisan, as commanded in the book of the Law."

"That's right, Hilkiah," Josiah answered. "It will be the first official celebration of Passover since the time of my great-grandfather Hezekiah."

"It will be wonderful to have Passover again," commented an older priest, "and the Feast of Unleavened Bread, too."

"I've read about this feast in the book of the Law, and of its meaning in the history of our people." Shaphan smiled. "What a privilege to have an opportunity to take part in it."

"Many of our people will be too poor to provide a lamb for their feast," Ahikam observed. "We will need to do something to help them . . . so that everyone can participate."

The king thought to himself a moment. "Let me know how many people you think are in this situation. We'll see what we can do."

"We'll need to teach the people that they should put away all yeast out of their houses before the Passover," Hilkiah commented. "And then they'll need to keep their homes cleared of leavening until after the seven days of the Feast of Unleavened Bread."

"That's right," one of the other priests commented. "We'll need to show them how to do this."

"I know that the book of the Law excludes yeast from the houses of God's people during Passover," still another priest remarked. "But why does God want us to do it?"

"Yeast is a symbol of sin," Shaphan explained, turning to face the questioner. "As yeast penetrates throughout the dough and affects every part, just so sin spreads throughout our minds and affects every part of our thinking and doing. By putting all yeast out of our houses for the feast, we are exhibiting our desire to remove sin from our lives."

"Be sure to explain that to the people," Hilkiah suggested. "It will make the feast much more meaningful."

"I guess we have plenty to do." Josiah concluded. "Let's work on it and meet day after tomorrow to check on our progress."

"Well said," Hilkiah told him as they rose to leave.

"The Passover feast helps us to remember how Yahweh saved our people just before the Exodus," Shaphan, the priest-scribe, explained to the elders of the clans of Judah. Many others had joined them in the Temple court and sat cross-legged on the stone pavement.

"Just before the Exodus, when our people escaped from Egypt, God sent 10 plagues, one after another, to get Pharaoh to let God's people leave. But Pharaoh wouldn't budge, despite the plagues meant to encourage him to obey.

"The tenth plague threatened that the angel of death would fly over Egypt, killing all the firstborn of human beings and animals. 'Pharaoh will not let Israel, my firstborn, leave Egypt. So I will strike his firstborn that he may know that I am Yahweh, the God who created the world and all that is in it.'

"Yahweh didn't want His people to suffer the death of their firstborn"—Shaphan cleared his throat before continuing—"so He asked them to do something that would save them from the plague. God commanded that each household should kill a lamb and roast it whole—with its entrails still in the body. The members of the family were to be dressed for travel, with their sandals on their feet and their staves in their hands.

"Here's the most important part," the priest went on. "When they killed the lamb, they were to take some of its blood and paint it on the doorposts and on the lintel over the door. God promised, 'When I see the blood, I will pass over you.' That's where the name of the feast comes from. And God asked us to continue to practice this for all generations to come."

"Why haven't we done this before?" one of the elders asked.

"Our people have worshipped idols, burned their children to Molech, the detestable god of the Ammonites; they worshipped on every high hill, and paid obeisance to the sun, and moon, and stars." Shaphan sought to make it as clear as possible. "Since Yahweh's people refused to worship Him as He commanded, they had also stopped observing the feasts and rituals that Yahweh wanted them to observe."

"How are the preparations coming?" Josiah asked as the priests gathered before him.

"We are pleased to report that the people have a real desire to return to Yahweh," Hilkiah, the high priest, reported. "God's people want to worship Him in all the ways He has ordained. They are willing to make all the preparations necessary for the Passover."

"Have you found any who will be unable to afford a lamb for their family's meal?" the king inquired.

"Yes, we have," Ahikam answered. "It's a large number, but I found that there are about 30,000 families who won't be able to take part in the Passover meal unless they have some outside help."

"H'mmm. I believe I can give that many lambs out of the royal flocks. Perhaps other supplies the people will need can be cared for from the Temple treasury."

"That's a generous gift, Your Majesty," Shaphan blurted in surprise. "God will bless you for such a wonderful gift." He turned to Hilkiah. "I believe that we can care for the other needs from the Temple treasury, don't you think?"

"I'm sure we can."

"Let's get together again day after tomorrow . . . to make sure everything is ready."

As the priests rose and filed out of the room, Jedidah emerged from a side entrance. "That was a magnanimous gift, my son."

"I love Yahweh with all my heart," returned Josiah. He continued to sit in the royal chair. "It's a small thing to help His people celebrate the feast as He wants them to."

Jedidah smiled and bent over to kiss her son on the forehead. "God bless you, my king."

The fourteenth of Nisan arrived, and each family removed all yeast from its household premises, killed the Passover lamb, dabbed blood on the doorposts and the lintel over the door, and roasted their lamb whole. They ate it while dressed as if for a journey, with sandals on their feet and their walking sticks in their hands.

On the following day, a special Sabbath, the Jews celebrated the first day of the Feast of Unleavened Bread. On the third day after Passover, farmers brought the first cuttings of their barley harvest, and the priest waved them before the

Lord (the "wave sheaf," or "firstfruits"). The festival continued for another five days.

With the participation of the people, the generosity of
the leaders, the instruction the people received day after day,
and the closeness that everyone felt to Yahweh—it turned
out to be the greatest Passover since the time of Samuel!

Chapter 10

The Invasion

"Jeremiah is here to see you, Your Majesty." A servant stood in the doorway to the king's private chambers.

"Yes, please show him in."

The prophet bowed to show his respect to the leader of his nation. "I have a message from Yahweh to share with you."

Josiah motioned to a seat. "I'm always happy to receive word from God." Josiah marveled that Yahweh had singled him out.

"God is pleased with your attempts at reform, and many will be won to the way of God because of your efforts. But . . ." Jeremiah hesitated, not because he was afraid to give the message, but because he knew it would bring sorrow to his friend, the king.

"But . . .?" Josiah echoed.

"But the reformation will not bring most of the people to God. What you see as repentance by the majority of the people is only a superficial one. It has not really turned their hearts away from idolatry."

"The people still practice idolatry?" The king's hands began to tremble.

"They do." Jeremiah glanced upward. "God said: 'Be appalled at this, O heavens, and shudder with great horror. My people have committed two sins: They have forsaken me, the spring of living water, and have dug their own cisterns, broken cisterns that cannot hold water.'" He shifted in his seat, and looked into Josiah's eyes. "Yahweh has taken Judah to

Himself as His wife, His chosen people. And yet they have been unfaithful to Him."

Then Jeremiah began to pace about the room. "God has said: 'Have you seen what faithless Israel has done? She has gone up on every high hill and under every spreading tree and has committed adultery there. I thought that after she had done all this she would return to me, but she did not, and her unfaithful sister Judah saw it. I gave faithless Israel her certificate of divorce and sent her away because of all her adulteries. Yet I saw that her unfaithful sister Judah had no fear; she also went out and committed adultery. Because Israel's immorality mattered so little to her, she defiled the land and committed adultery with stone and wood. In spite of all this, her unfaithful sister Judah did not return to me with all her heart, but only in pretense.'"

Josiah wept, tears streaming down his face and into his beard. "Has all I've done for Yahweh been for naught?" he exclaimed. "Is there no hope?"

"You remember the prophecy of Huldah, at the time when the scroll was discovered in the Temple? It is true. You will die in peace, but the Lord will destroy this nation because of its wickedness."

Jeremiah began to pace the room again. "You have destroyed the evil places of worship. But you do not see what they are doing in the towns of Judah and in the streets of Jerusalem. Yahweh has shown me that the children gather wood, the fathers light the fire, and the women knead the dough and make cakes of bread for the Queen of Heaven. They pour out drink offerings to other gods to provoke Yahweh to anger. But am I the one they are provoking? declares the Lord. Are they not rather harming themselves, to their own shame?"

"Yahweh told you that?"

"Yes." Jeremiah hung his head and sat down. "But there

is more." He looked at Josiah again. "The iniquity in the days of Manasseh was so brazen that to permit it to pass without punishment will not work for the future good of the nation. Even if the present generation is apparently repentant, and seeks to effect reforms, future generations, who will learn that the flagrant iniquity and idolatry of a previous generation had been permitted without rebuke—will be emboldened in sin. Unfortunately, also, the reforms that you have made have affected only the majority superficially.

"'Therefore this is what the Sovereign Lord says: 'My anger and my wrath will be poured out on this place, on man and beast, on the trees of the field and on the fruit of the ground, and it will burn and not be quenched. For when I brought your forefathers out of Egypt and spoke to them, I did not just give them commands about burnt offerings and sacrifices, but I gave them this command: Obey me, and I will be your God and you will be my people. Walk in all the ways I command you, that it may go well with you.'"

"Again I ask, Jeremiah: Is there no hope for us?"

As the prophet stared into Josiah's face he saw the anguish of a man who had put all his heart into bringing reform to the nation. Tears streaked down his own cheeks as well. He wanted with all his heart to bring good news to his friend. "If the people really change their ways and their actions and deal with each other justly, if they do not oppress the alien, the fatherless, or the widow and do not shed innocent blood in this place, and if they do not follow other gods to their own harm, then I will let you live in this place, in the land I gave your forefathers for ever and ever, says the Lord."

Then the prophet smiled. "There is hope for those who turn to Yahweh and His salvation." A grimace flashed across his face. "But for those who refuse to follow God, there is no hope. And for the nation . . . it will come to an end. But not in your time."[1]

"This would be a good time to annex the area that used to be the kingdom of Israel," the prime minister commented in a council meeting soon after the Feast of Unleavened Bread.

"That's right," Shaphan added. "The Assyrians took most of the people into captivity, and those still left in the land aren't really organized into a nation."

"That seems feasible," Josiah mused. "We'd certainly not meet with any resistance."

"I feel this is necessary," the prime minister continued, "because there are still many pagan shrines and local altars left in that area. If we're to do a complete job of bringing our nation back to God, we need to include our kin to the north as well."

"I agree," Hilkiah responded. "As long as there are pagan altars and high places, those who desire to worship idols will travel north to those sites. We really must extend our reform to all of the Promised Land."

"I think it's a good idea." Josiah thought a moment. "I've always wished we could somehow give them an opportunity to participate fully in worshipping Yahweh."

"Then it's agreed to do this?" the prime minister asked.

"Yes," finalized the king.

"Another thing we need to remember," Shaphan put in. "The law of God specifies that all the priests and Levites should perform their official duties *within* the Temple gates here in Jerusalem."

Josiah smiled. "We'll keep that in mind as we come across Levites in the countryside during our campaign."

The commanding general frowned. "Because we have no idea what resistance we may encounter, we'll have to take a sizable force." He crossed his arms. "There might even be some Assyrian stragglers left behind."

"You're right," the king acknowledged. "As I see it, we're out to accomplish two goals: one, to rid the entire land of Israel—as God once called the territory of all the tribes—of all idolatrous practices. In doing that, we'll center all worship on the Temple here in Jerusalem. And two, we can extend the power of Judah, and more than double our territory."

"And it would exalt your power as ruler of all Israel," the commanding general smiled. "You'd be like David and Solomon!"

"I don't care about the power," Josiah snapped. "My goal is to bring all Israel back to Yahweh. Extending my 'power,' as you call it, is only a means to accomplish this goal."

Josiah and his military leaders assembled a sizable army in the open area on the heights north of the city. Even though Shaphan's position was that of second priest and official scribe, he also served as a general in the army. He commanded the brigade comprising men from the area of Gibea, Ramah, Geba, and Anathoth, a sizable group numbering more than 1,000 men. Other brigades added their soldiers to the army—which grew to more than 10,000 men.

"We won't use force against any city or town, unless we meet considerable resistance," the king explained. "And then we'll use only enough to put down the resistance. Keep tight rein on your men. I don't want any pillaging or assaults on individuals. Shaphan's men will deal with pagan priests and the high places, so you won't have to be concerned about that."

"Why are you taking such a large force?" one of the officers inquired.

"We probably won't need an army this size," the king

explained, "except that we don't really know what we might encounter."

"Will we engage any Assyrians?" another questioned.

"My scouts report no Assyrian forces in the area, but we're prepared in case they appear." Josiah stood in his chariot and surveyed the army. "I think everything is in order now. My personal guard and I will lead the way."

Josiah instructed his charioteer as to the route they would take, and then lifted his spear to signal the advance. As the army moved out, one unit at a time, it began to have the appearance of a living thing, snaking its way along the roads that led toward the north.

Shaphan repeatedly sent squads out to destroy pagan shrines or high places. They executed all those connected with them, often burning their bodies on the altars of their high places, using wood acquired from an Ashtoreth pole or other wooden cult objects for the fires. The presence of human bones at the shrine would destroy its "sacredness" forever in the eyes of the people.

Having no specific battle plan, Josiah led the army gently, traveling at a slow enough pace so as to keep the troops from becoming fatigued. Every two hours Josiah had the men stop and rest. He wanted his army to be fresh and rested should they meet any heavy resistance—or a foreign army.

The army approached Bethel, where Jeroboam—the first king of Israel at the beginning of the divided monarchy—had built a temple around the image of a golden calf. Giving orders that the army make camp outside of the city, he led Shaphan and a group of his men into the city, to the pagan temple. They destroyed it and its golden calf, as they had done all the other shrines and high places.

Then Josiah looked around, and when he saw the tombs

dotting the hillside, he had the bones removed from them and burned on the altar to defile it.

"What is that tombstone I see?" Josiah asked at one point.

"It marks the tomb of the man of God who came from Judah and pronounced against the altar of Bethel the very things you have done to it," some of the men of the city told him.

"Leave it alone," the king said. "Don't let anyone disturb his bones." So they spared his tomb.[2]

Josiah now remembered his mother telling him about the prophet.

Centuries before, God had sent someone from Judah to Bethel. The man arrived just as Jeroboam stood by the altar ready to make an offering. Interrupting the ceremony, the prophet declared, "O altar, altar! This is what the Lord says: A son named Josiah will be born to the house of David. On you he will sacrifice the priests of the high places who now make offerings here, and human bones will be burned on you."

The man of God also announced what would confirm the validity of the prophecy: "This is the sign the Lord has declared: The altar will be split apart and the ashes on it will be poured out."

When King Jeroboam heard what the prophet from Judah proclaimed against the altar at Bethel, he stretched out his hand from the altar and said, "Seize him!" But his hand immediately shriveled, so that he could not pull it back. Also, the altar suddenly split apart, its ashes pouring onto the ground just as the prophet had predicted.

Then Jeroboam turned to the man of God and pled, "Intercede with the Lord your God and pray for me that my hand may be restored." When the prophet did, the king's hand became normal again.[3]

"And so the prophecy has been fulfilled," Josiah commented to Shaphan. "As illogical as it may seem to human thinking, the prophecy made by the man of God more than 350 years ago has come true—just as he said it would."

"Yahweh is a mighty God," Shaphan replied. "He knows the end from the beginning, and to Him, the future is as open as if it were today."

❧

Still moving at a measured pace, Josiah's army zigzagged across the old northern kingdom. Coming to the city of Samaria, Ahab's old capital, they destroyed numerous altars and high places, including many shrines to Baal, the god of the Sidonians—and of Jezebel.

Then continuing on, the Judean force ranged through the territories of Manasseh, Ephraim, Simeon, and as far as Naphtali. Heading west, they came to the ruins of the fortress city of Megiddo.

"This is an excellent site to set up defenses to protect us from invasion, especially from the north and the west," Josiah observed as he scanned the area.

"I agree," the commanding general said, also studying the landscape. "That's the reason countless kings have fortified this place through the centuries." He walked around the site. The Assyrians rebuilt some of the city, while other parts still lie in ruins. Then he pointed to a section where erosion had uncovered previous structures. "As you can see, there are several layers of cities under the present ruins."

The Carmel Pass to the west opened to the Way of the Kings—a highway used for centuries by both merchants and kings. East of the pass sprawled the Valley of Megiddo, also known as the Valley of Jezreel.

"I can see why the city was built here," Josiah remarked. "This valley would make an excellent battlefield."

The Temple Gates

The king stepped down from his chariot and strode around the city, followed by the commanding general. "Look how massive these walls are, and those gates must have been nearly impossible to break through."

He studied the gates for several moments. Each was a long narrow passageway overshadowed by walls on both sides. A withering volley of arrows would have greeted anyone who sought to attack them. At the end of the entrance, the passageway came to an abrupt end, with the city gates inset to the right and the left. The enemy couldn't use a battering ram on the gates, because there wasn't enough room for such a device. And no one could have long survived in the gateway, because of the arrows from the defenders.

"I'd think such gates would be unconquerable."

"Anyone who conquered the city would have to break into it some other way," the general commented.

Josiah stared at the gate for some time. "I want you to work with the royal architects and draw up the plans for strengthening this fortress," he said after a while. "Perhaps we don't need such a large city, because only the defenders and their families will live here."

"I'll have my military engineers work with your draftsmen," the officer replied.

After several months' absence, the army returned to Jerusalem, and the men to their homes. "We've accomplished several things," Josiah told his mother and wives. The children sat, wide-eyed, in a circle at his feet. "We wiped out the shrines and high places of the northern kingdom. But we also extended the borders of Judah all the way north to Megiddo, and west to the Great Sea. We have the largest and most powerful kingdom this side of Egypt."

"Well, don't let it go to your head," Zebidah chided.

"You may be a powerful king, but you are still my husband, and a child of Yahweh."

"That's right," laughed Hamutal. "The most humble child of God is just as important to the Lord as you are, my husband."

"It's dangerous to speak of things that *we've* accomplished," Jedidah cautioned. "There's no surer way to get God angry. It's as bad as idolatry."

"I get the point," the king replied, his face pink with embarrassment. "Thank you for reminding me of my place." He sighed. "It's true. I may be king, but that's really just a position that God has given me. I can use it as a way of serving Him, or as something to inspire an evil heart—as my father and grandfather did." A tear trickled down his cheek, and he swiped at it. "I'm grateful that God has given me the privilege of doing what He has called me to do. But I would be just as grateful to work for God as one who sweeps the Temple courts."

---

[1] Jeremiah's message to Josiah is taken, in part, from Jeremiah 2:12, 13, NIV; 3:1-12, NIV; 7:17-27, NIV.

[2] 2 Kings 23:16-18, NIV.

[3] 1 Kings 13:1-6, NIV.

Chapter 11

Cities and Towns

"We were unopposed during the entire campaign," Josiah told the royal council. It had grown in number since the king had invited Jeremiah, Zephaniah, and Habakkuk to become advisers. "We now have control over most of the territory once governed by David and Solomon."

"That's wonderful," the prime minister grinned. "Finally the rebellion that Jeroboam started has been brought to an end."

"We had very little to do with it," Jeremiah reminded them. "The Assyrians left the country wide open for the taking. Yahweh made it possible for us to step into the void the enemy left by pulling out their army."

"That's true," the king nodded. "God has blessed us by giving us control over it."

"And He gave us the courage to rid the area of idolatry, too," Shaphan added.

"Amen," the rest chorused.

"That's a large area to govern," the prime minister observed. "Have you considered how to protect it?"

"Yes," Josiah replied. "We'll need to station garrisons in all the fortress cities. Most of them need little repair. All we need to do is to step in and take them over."

"Which cities are we talking about?" the commanding general questioned.

"Beth-shemesh, Shechem, Gezer, Hazor, and Tirzah," the king listed. "And, of course, Megiddo."

"We really need a fortress city down by the Great Sea," the commanding general suggested. "Perhaps in the area of Mezad."

"That's a good idea." Josiah stared at the ceiling a moment. "Perhaps we should send survey crews to these sites to find out what kind of additional work each city will need."

"And I'll organize garrisons to staff the existing fortresses," offered the commanding general.

"That's good. This is all we have time for today," Josiah announced. "It's nearly time for the evening sacrifice."

"I've sent a group of surveyors with a heavy guard," Joah, the royal recorder, reported to Josiah. "They'll examine the area around Mezad in order to decide where would be the best location for a fortress in that area. I've also sent a group to Megiddo to assess how best to consolidate that fortress."

"Good. You should also send surveyors to Gezer, Shechem, Beth-shemesh, and Tirzah to strengthen their walls and bulwarks."

Josiah wanted to be sure that the fortress cities would be able to withstand attacks from the massive armies often fielded by Egypt and the empires of Mesopotamia.

"If a fortress cannot stop an army," Josiah told Hamutal in her room that evening, "then it's of no use to us."

He had married Hamutal two years after his marriage to Zebidah as a political necessity, to assure that her city, Libnah, would remain loyal to His kingdom. The city lay only three miles from the border of Gaza, an area controlled by Egypt. The king intended to make Libnah one of his fortresses—to guard the highway that led from the coast up to the central highlands and Jerusalem.

In time he came to love Hamutal, just as he had learned

to love Zebidah. The two women had managed to become friends, and both adored Jedidah, the queen mother. Josiah felt he had been blessed to have such a happy family.

"That's true," Hamutal replied to his remark about the fortresses. "My father told me what happened during the reign of Hezekiah when the Assyrians destroyed Lachish. They would have overwhelmed Libnah, too, if it hadn't been for the loss of their army at Jerusalem."

"Grandfather described to me how God wiped out so many Assyrians in one night," Josiah replied. "But it must have been frightening for your people in Libnah!"

"It was," she gasped. "Hundreds of our soldiers were killed on the walls as they fought to defend our city. Two of my uncles perished in the war."

"I'm sorry. But at least the whole city was not destroyed."

"I guess you're right." She lay her head on his shoulder and sighed. "But still . . ."

Reports came regularly from those surveying the different cities. "Your Majesty, Hazor needs very little work," a messenger announced. "Its walls have been rebuilt since the Assyrian invasion, and are sufficient to defend the city. Seventy-five cubits in height and about 45 cubits thick, they are of stone on the outside and reinforced on the inside with mud brick. It looks as though at some time in the past the houses that had been built next to the wall have been removed in order to have better access to it. The military engineers felt this was a good arrangement."

Pausing to clear his throat, the messenger glanced at the pavement, then back to the king. "It seems that at one time the walls were hollow, with rooms for warehouses and shops. But the space has been filled in so as to provide greater strength. The gates appear to be in order as well, my lord."

"Very good," Josiah stated. "Take word that I'm pleased to know about their findings. Tell me more about the gates."

Many city gates had towers with six chambers that provided rooms for business and legal matters, and for garrison space needed by guards and defenders. Such a gateway was the first line of defense, as it would be the first area an enemy would attack. Battlements that jutted out from the wall flanked it on each side. Defenders stationed there would be in position to shoot arrows or hurl stones at anyone approaching the gate.

During peacetime the area outside the gate served as a gathering place for merchants. Craftsmen, farmers, bakers, potters, leather workers, and tailors set up booths and stalls there. Traders sold jewelry from Egypt, Phoenician furnishings, perfumes from Arabia, and ingots of metal from Cyprus and Anatolia.

The gate area also became a courthouse when people needed legal documents prepared or had to deal with criminal activity. Communal executions of criminals took place there as well. Such criminal justice helped the people realize that crime was not just an individual matter: it endangered the entire community.

At the gate, too, judges heard testimonies and announced their decisions in all matters public or private. All of their decisions were based on ancient law. Among the various crimes of murder, theft, and idolatry, however, one of the most nefarious involved a judge who perverted justice in order to receive bribes. Such a person, when found out, received execution.

The city itself, with a few exceptions, had a fortress of only a few acres. The only people who actually lived within the walls were the local governor and his officials. Everyone else had to build their houses outside the fortress walls. They would flee into it only during times of invasion. Often the sections outside the walls became so much a part of the city that walls had to be extended around them for their protection. Hazor enlarged its walls so that, eventually, the city grew to more than 200 acres.

Inside the walled fortress, room was at a premium. It had little open space for public assembly and market activity. Any open area in the city could usually be found in front of important buildings, such as the city hall, or near the gate. (Hezekiah had marshaled his troops in an open place near the East Gate when hostile armies approached.)

The majority of the people, though, lived in small, unwalled villages. They had more community space than cities, as they were not restricted by the city walls. The people in the towns farmed the surrounding land and, on occasion, took their produce to the markets of larger towns.

Lacking any substantial timber supply, people constructed their houses of stone and mud plaster. The entrance led to an open courtyard, which served, among other things, as an open-air kitchen. Flanking the courtyard were two rooms with cobblestone floors for the family's domestic animals, and two slightly smaller rooms for the family itself. Across the back of the house stretched a living room, often six by 21 feet. Wooden ceiling beams supported a second floor, reached by a ladder and used for sleeping. Another ladder allowed the family to go up onto the roof, where they stored grain and oil in jars. In the summer families could sleep on the roof to catch a welcome breeze. All the houses were of uniform size and layout.

The entrance into a city house usually led into an alleyway, and often stairs on the outside of the house led to the roof. If the house sat next to a city wall, the stairs would be built against the wall.

Sanitary conditions were very unhealthy everywhere. Homes had poor ventilation. Decayed food and feces coupled with the heat frequently caused disease. People often burned frankincense and other sweet-smelling substances to keep down the offending odors and drive away insects.

People dumped dung and other waste in the streets, and in some of the larger cities civil servants made a living collecting it and disposing of it into a communal dung heap—usually outside the city. The houses of some of the wealthier people had stone-lined drainage systems for sewage and excess rainwater. But they then poured their contents into the streets.

The higher class usually lived in the western part of town. It allowed them to catch the prevailing winds, which would carry their smoke and odors away. But these wafted over the rest of the town, polluting the air even more. Western houses were also much larger and built of better materials than those of the poor. They had pillars with stone foundations, and a few window openings. A central courtyard contained the oven and cooking storage jars, and often became a gathering area for family and friends.

Since space was so precious, streets were no more than narrow paths between buildings, sometimes ending in blind alleys. Pedestrian traffic, carts, booths, and accumulated garbage often choked them.

At the larger markets in Jerusalem, Lachish, Megiddo, and Hazor people could buy all kinds of things. Most farm families tried to visit them at least once or twice a year.

Families enjoyed a number of yearly holidays. When observed, the people ate the Passover meal at home. Scripture required the men had to visit Jerusalem three times a year to celebrate important religious holidays. The Feast of Unleavened Bread began on the morning after Passover and lasted for a full week. The Feast of Weeks, often called Pentecost, commenced 50 days later, at the beginning of grain harvest. The Feast of Tabernacles, in the middle of the seventh month, took place at the close of the olive and fruit harvest, and became a festive occasion in Jerusalem. People used tree branches and other materials to make simple shelters—tabernacles—in which to stay for the holiday. It reminded them of the 40 years that Israel had lived in tents while wanderers in the wilderness.

Such feasts were often family affairs, filled with travel, good food, and Temple ritual. They permitted children and adults to make new friends from other places in Judah. Also they allowed the entire family to learn from the Levites, who taught them about the law.

"I like going to Jerusalem," a girl told her mother as they walked toward home. "There are so many things to do, and other children to play with."

"Yes," her mother replied, smiling. "And I learned a lot more about how important it is to be faithful to Yahweh."

"That's right," the father added. "When they sacrificed the lamb, I couldn't help thinking that the poor creature died for my sins."

"But doesn't the lamb represent the coming Messiah?" asked their oldest son.

"Yes."

"Will Messiah die for our sins?"

"I don't know." The man seemed puzzled. "It doesn't make sense to me, but . . . I guess God's ways are beyond our understanding."

"That's true," Mother said. "So very true."

Chapter 12

The Temple Gates

"Zebidah, Hamutal," Josiah called, "let's go to the Temple to worship. Mother, you are welcome too."

"Coming," the women returned, almost in unison.

"I am with you, my son," Jedidah beamed. "It will be good to bow in the presence of Yahweh again."

"You bowed 'in the presence of Yahweh' just last evening," Hamutal commented.

"Yes, but just twice a day seems so little to me. I feel as did David, that I would like to be in His presence always."

"Sometimes my feeling too," the king replied. "And yet, as we do the work He has given us to do, we are always in His presence."

The four quietly entered the Temple court through the Palace Gate. His wives and mother turned toward the women's court, while Josiah headed to the place reserved for the king.

As Josiah knelt facing the Temple, the sun rose behind him. *God doesn't want us to worship the sun.* His mind reflected on the situation. *So He set the Temple facing east so as we worship Him we'll not be bowing to the sun.* Sun worship had become a major part of almost all the religions of the surrounding nations.

Before him, on either side of the Temple entrance, stood two bronze pillars: "Jakin" on the south and "Boaz" on the north. Each pillar stood 23.5 cubits (34.5 feet) high, including its capital. He remembered how he had been anointed king while he stood before Boaz.

A priest appeared, leading a year-old lamb, a beautiful animal, since it had no blemishes at all. *The lamb represents the coming Messiah, who will be perfect in every way,* Josiah reflected.

The priest brought the lamb to the side of the altar of burnt offering, a massive bronze structure on which a fire burned continually. (The priests kept it going day and night as a reminder of the pillar of cloud and of fire that led the Israelites through the wilderness, and of God's constant presence with them now.)

Josiah watched the priest slit the lamb's throat, and, as the creature slumped to the ground, the priest caught its blood in a golden bowl. Setting the bowl aside, he lifted the lamb, climbed the steps to the altar, and laid the animal onto the fire. The choir sang, from the Psalms of David, of God's love and care for His people, and of His coming Messiah, who would free the world from sin.

Retracing his steps, the priest dipped his finger into the blood and sprinkled some at the base of the altar. He then took the bowl into the holy place of the Temple, and wiped some of the blood on the horns of the small altar of incense that stood before the veil that separated the holy place from the Most Holy Place. Incense on this small altar drifted upward day and night, a fitting symbol of the prayers of God's people and of the intercession of the Messiah for His people. The sweet smell drifted over the veil into the Most Holy Place, and out of the Temple over the worshippers.

When the priest emerged from the Temple again, the kneeling congregation resounded, in chorus, "Amen." Then they rose and went home to begin their daily duties.

Josiah met his wives and his mother after the service, and together they exited through the Royal Gate. As they did so he glanced at the gate. "Go into the palace," he told the women on impulse. "I want to look at these gates more closely."

As the women drifted away, Josiah ran his hand over the smooth surface of one of the gates. "Suddenly a splinter stabbed into his hand. He worked for a minute or two, trying to extract it.

"May I help you?"

The voice startled him. He looked up to see the prophet Habakkuk strolling toward him. "Perhaps you can." The king felt a bit sheepish. "I've gotten a splinter from the gate, and I can't seem to get it out."

The prophet approached and took Josiah's hand in his. Looking closely, he pushed his thumbnail under the opening of the wound where the sliver had entered, and with his other thumb he pressed his nail deep into the heel of Josiah's palm and manipulated the fragment of wood toward the opening. Soon one end of the splinter appeared, and Habakkuk pulled it out. "Sometimes it takes two hands." He smiled.

"Thank you, Habakkuk. If I had you around always, I would need no physician. And to what do I owe the pleasure of your visit?"

"Your Majesty," he began, "I have noticed that all of the gates of the Temple are in a similar condition as this one, perhaps even worse. They look all right from a distance, but they are worn from the weather and from the continual handling of the gatekeepers." The prophet pointed to the area from which the king's splinter had come. "And the hinges of some of the gates are beginning to show extreme wear, many to the point that they could soon break."

"I appreciate your calling this to my attention. Perhaps it's time we repaired them. What would you suggest?"

"Well . . . we will need to make sure the Temple treasury has enough money to pay for these repairs. Then we must place an order with the metalworkers for hinges and other hardware, and to make an agreement with carpenters to construct the wooden doors."

"Let's go to Hilkiah and get his advice," the king suggested.

The two strode side by side toward the small room the high priest used as an office. Hilkiah sat on a stool, leaning over a table on which he had unrolled a copy of the book of the Law. He glanced up when the men came to the door. "Come in, Your Majesty, Habakkuk." Hustling into an adjoining room, he brought out two more stools.

As he and the prophet had made themselves comfortable, the king spoke: "Habakkuk and I have noticed that the gates of the Temple are in disrepair and need replacing."

"Yes. I've seen that too," Hilkiah replied. "How do you suggest we solve the problem?"

"We were wondering," Habakkuk said, "if there is enough money in the Temple treasury to pay for such an expensive project."

"I don't know," the high priest confessed. "Let me ask the treasurer." Rising from his table, Hilkiah left the room and hurried down the row of other rooms to the chamber of the treasurer. Some minutes later he returned with a smile. "Yes, I think we have enough. We must keep a reserve to cover the expenses of the Levites, and for other needs that arise from time to time, but . . . yes . . . let's do it."

"I know just the man to oversee the work," Habakkuk suggested. "He seems to be the best builder in the city, and others look to him for leadership in projects like this."

"Then seek him out," Josiah said. "Show him what needs to be done, and negotiate with him on the price he'll need to complete the task."

During the next several weeks workmen moved about the Temple gates, measuring them, observing the placement of each one, how it swung on its hinges, how one leaf met with the other, and what special considerations each set required. They made templates of the carvings originally made on the gates by placing papyri sheets over them and pressing a flattened edge of metal over its surface—thus leaving an image of the carving on the papyri. The work would all be done in their shops, for they knew they should not use a tool within the Temple area.

Before long, the gates were finished and ready to be hung. Josiah, his wives and mother, and many townspeople came to observe. The craftsmen had to ask some of the onlookers to make way so that they had room to do their work.

The metalworkers removed the huge bolts that held the old wooden leaves to the hinges. "Careful now," one of the carpenters warned. "These gate are extremely heavy. Don't let them fall on you. We don't want anyone to get hurt." Several of his fellow laborers took hold of a huge old door as it fell away from the hinges and lowered it onto a waiting cart so they could take it away. Then the metalworkers removed the hinges from the posts.

"The new hinges should fit in the same places where the old hinges were," one of the metalworkers explained as they began to mount them on the gateposts. Soon they had the new hinges secured.

"Up," called the foreman of the carpenters as they lifted the new door. "Shift it this way . . . now stand it up . . . move it to the gatepost . . . block it up, so the hinges will fit the holes . . . good."

The metalworkers bolted the new doors into place, then went to the next gate. The finished gates opened with so little effort that one man could swing them either way.

"Most of the workmen wanted to contribute toward the new gates," Habakkuk told Josiah as the king sat on his throne. "So replacing them cost less than we had originally figured."

The Temple Gates

"Wonderful." Josiah stood and walked down the six steps of the throne, throwing his arms around the prophet in a warm embrace, then holding Habakkuk at arm's length. "Please express my thankfulness to the workers. And I appreciate your efforts, too."

"I am sure that Yahweh is pleased that we have repaired the Temple gates," the older man observed. "He will bless us because of this expression of our love to Him."

Chapter 13

The Quiet Invasion

Staring out the window into the drizzling rain, Josiah clutched his robes around himself and stood near the brazier for warmth. Rumors from the south had unsettled him, and now that he had discovered that they were true, he felt a growing anger. And yet, however frustrated he felt, he couldn't find any way to solve the situation.

The Arab tribes of Edom had been moving north. Farmers, craftsmen, people from all walks of life, had migrated north to settle in the Negev—an expansive, hilly region in the southern part of Judah, bordering Gaza in the west, and fading into the desert of Sin far to the south. Although Manasseh and now Josiah had constructed numerous settlements there, the number of foreign immigrants had increased at an alarming rate. So many Edomites had flocked into the region's towns and villages that in many places they now dominated.

The Edomite majorities had brought in their customs and idolatrous religions. As the Judahite population continued to leave the more southern regions, some entire towns no longer had a Jew in them. The climate of the Negev seemed much less harsh than that of the territory that the Arabs had come from, so it especially attracted them.

"Edom is *not* attacking us!" The prime minister pounded his fist on the table in the council chamber. "And we can't stop people from moving from one town to the next, even if they *are* Edomites."

"I know, I know." Ahikam grew irritated at the man.

"But isn't it possible that we could more carefully control those whom we allow to immigrate into our country?"

"It would be nice if we could." The king sought to bring peace once again to the council. "But I don't see how we could do that, short of having military officials at the gate of every city, town, or village. We can't erect a fortress all the way from the sea to the Sinai desert! And I'm equally unsure that we would be wise to spread our troops out over such a vast area. It would greatly weaken the army, and we have to maintain a strong military base here so that we're ready to defend our kingdom should we be attacked."

"I agree with His Majesty," responded the commanding general who arose, unconsciously stood at attention, and bowed to the king. After seating himself once more, he turned to the council. "We need to keep our soldiers close enough to Jerusalem so that we could put a large force in the field, should one of our closer neighbors show hostility toward us."

"Do we even know how many villages are involved?" Shaphan enjoyed working with statistics. "Maybe the problem isn't as broad as we see it. Perhaps we're reacting to what could turn out to be no more than roaches in a cupboard."

The council laughed at the comparison of Edomites to roaches. But it seemed appropriate under the present situation.

"Well then," the prime minister responded, "it might be a good thing to send out a fact-finding mission to visit the towns in the Negev and report back to us what they discover. At that point, then, we would be able to make a more informed decision."

"See to it," Josiah ordered.

The rain still fell as the men left the palace. Pulling their shawls over their heads to protect themselves, they scattered across the city.

As Josiah entered the royal family's private quarters, Eliakim, his oldest son, ran up; Shulum and Mattaniah,

Hamutal's sons, following closely behind. "Come, Father, look at what we made." They seemed full of excitement over the novelty of their homemade toy.

"I'll have to look at it another time," Josiah told them. "I need to think over the matters we discussed in the council meeting."

The monarch didn't see the disappointment in his sons' eyes. It seemed that he was always involved with this or that at the palace, and didn't think he had time to play with the children. He had not yet learned that the best time to spend with them occurred the moment they wanted his attention—even if only for a few minutes.

Soon it came time to go to the evening sacrifice. Jedidah, Zebidah, Hamutal, and a small parade of sons and daughters approached Josiah. He was startled when he realized that he had lost track of the time. But he examined his children carefully, eyeing them to make sure each had dressed for worship in the rain. As they emerged from the royal residence the king blinked as the raindrops struck his cheeks and eyelashes.

"Why do we have to go out in the rain?" one of the girls complained. "It seems that we could worship at home. Why go to the Temple in the rain?"

"We go to the Temple because God is there," Hamutal, the child's mother, explained. "God wants us to go before Him morning and evening to witness the sacrifice of the lamb."

"That's right," her father added. "And the service teaches us about how much our sin hurts God."

Eliakim wrinkled up his nose. "I don't see anything about God in burning lambs, sprinkling blood, and burning incense. Besides, all the other religions do that too."

They passed the new gates that separated the Temple from the palace.

"Don't say such things," Zebidah scolded. "Now all of you be quiet."

The Temple Gates

The service proceeded as usual. But at the time that the high priest emerged from the Temple to bless the people, Habakkuk the prophet rose and prayed:

> "Lord, I have heard of your fame;
> I stand in awe of your deeds, O Lord.
> Renew them in our day,
>   in our time make them known;
>   in wrath remember mercy.
> God came from Teman,
>   the Holy One from Mount Paran.
> His glory covered the heavens
>   and his praise filled the earth.
> His splendor was like the sunrise;
>   rays flashed from his hand,
>   where his power was hidden.
> Plague went before him;
>   pestilence followed his steps.
> He stood, and shook the earth;
>   he looked, and made the nations tremble.
> The ancient mountains crumbled
>   and the age-old hills collapsed.
> His ways are eternal.
> I saw the tents of Cushan in distress,
>   the dwellings of Midian in anguish.
> Were you angry with the rivers, O Lord?
> Was your wrath against the streams?
> Did you rage against the sea
>   when you rode with your horses
>   and your victorious chariots?
> You uncovered your bow,
>   you called for many arrows.
> You split the earth with rivers;
>   the mountains saw you and writhed.

Torrents of water swept by;
>   the deep roared and lifted its waves on high.
Sun and moon stood still in the heavens
>   at the glint of your flying arrows,
>   at the lightning of your flashing spear.
In wrath you strode through the earth
>   and in anger you threshed the nations.
You came out to deliver your people,
>   to save your anointed one.
You crushed the leader of the land of wickedness,
>   you stripped him from head to foot.
With his own spear you pierced his head
>   when his warriors stormed out to scatter us,
>   gloating as though about to devour
>   the wretched who were in hiding.
You trampled the sea with your horses,
>   churning the great waters.
I heard and my heart pounded,
>   my lips quivered at the sound;
>   decay crept into my bones,
>   and my legs trembled.
Yet I will wait patiently for the day of calamity
>   to come on the nation invading us.
Though the fig tree does not bud
>   and there are no grapes on the vines,
>   though the olive crop fails
>   and the fields produce no food,
>   though there are no sheep in the pen
>   and no cattle in the stalls,
>   yet I will rejoice in the Lord,
>   I will be joyful in God my Savior.
The Sovereign Lord is my strength;
>   he makes my feet like the feet of a deer,
>   he enables me to go on the heights."*

The Temple Gates

Josiah felt humbled at the words. Though there was much that he did not understand, he heard the sound of God's voice in the mention of "the nation invading us" and other statements. The refrain especially comforted him:

> "Yet I will rejoice in the Lord,
>   I will be joyful in God my Savior.
> The Sovereign Lord is my strength;
>   he makes my feet like the feet of a deer,
>   he enables me to go on the heights."

In a later council meeting Shaphan revealed the results of the Negev survey. "It is just as we feared," he intoned in the monotone style of most scribes as he read the report. "More and more of our towns in the Negev are really no longer *ours*. And those who still hold allegiance to us would be unable to stand alone should there be any hostilities in the area."

"With His Majesty's permission," the commanding general rumbled, "we will seek to put a stop to any move to immigrate further north."

"That seems like a wise thing to do," Josiah replied. "And perhaps we need to place some kind of military presence in the towns and settlements still loyal to us."

"Let me see your toy," Josiah offered when he arrived home that evening.

"Won't do any good now," Eliakim muttered. "You didn't really want to see it anyway, so we held a war and destroyed it."

"Yeah," mumbled Shalum. "We destroyed it."

If I'd only taken time to see it before, their father mused.

---

* Habakkuk 3:2-18, NIV.

Chapter 14

Egyptians Move North

"I'm having trouble with Eliakim," Zebidah complained to her husband. "His tutor saw him setting up a post behind the palace. He and his brothers and sisters went out and bowed down to it."

"Didn't anyone stop them?"

"Yes, his tutor disciplined Eliakim quite severely for it. He scolded the other children too. Eliakim said they were just 'playing games.'"

She took Josiah by the hand and looked directly into his eyes. Their gleam seemed hauntingly familiar . . . very much like when she had gazed at him on their wedding night. Such love they displayed! And yet . . . pleading.

"I know that you're very busy. A king can never get everything done that needs his attention. But please, won't you talk with him? And don't forget the others, too."

"I'll try. But I doubt he'll listen to me any more than he'll listen to you. If I'd spent more time with him when he was younger . . ."

"Yes, I know. He was such a good boy when he was younger . . ." Her voice trailed off as she remembered better times.

"But when he wanted my attention, I was always busy with something that seemed truly vital at the time. If only I had known then that the time to spend with children is when they want it, not necessarily when I want it."

"That's true, husband. But that time is gone, and now we

must try to make the best of what we have." She took him by both arms. "Please take time to talk to him. Maybe he'll listen to you."

Josiah searched for his son, and at last found him in the palace library, reading scrolls about the history of their people. "Why did Rehoboam act so stupidly?" Eliakim asked as his father sat down on a stool opposite him. "If he'd only listened to the elders and granted the leaders of the northern tribes their reasonable requests, we'd still have a united monarchy. And all those tribes that were taken captive would probably still be here."

"That's a good thought," his father remarked, impressed at his son's insight. "Suppose you were Rehoboam. All the elders came to you asking you to lower taxes and to reduce the enforced labor. You see that Jeroboam is in the group, and you know that he wants to be king. Also you know that he worships the gods of Egypt, and that if he becomes king, he'll lead the nation away from Yahweh. What would you do?"

"H'mmm." Eliakim had his elbow on the table and held his chin in the palm of his hand. He stared out of the window at the Mount of Olives. "I think I'd talk with those elders a little more and find out what they really want. It seems to me that Rehoboam didn't really listen to them enough to know what they had in mind."

"Ah, yes. Listening is important. What else would you do?"

"Well, I think I'd have my guard watch Jeroboam very carefully. The guy was trouble . . . even when he served Solomon."

"You're right there," Josiah mused. "The first thing he did when he got the 10 tribes to make him king was to lead them to worship idols."

The boy froze. He expected his father to launch into a speech about the evils of idol worship, to scold him for his own experimentation with idolatry. Regardless of what his father might say, he *felt* reprimanded. But the king didn't say anything about it. "What else would you have done?"

"I don't know." *I can see that my father knows about our game of worshipping idols the other day,* Eliakim thought. *Why else would he have mentioned it in regard to Jeroboam? But I dare not speak of it. I believe that there must be more power in the many gods that dwelt in the land before our people, more than just only one God, as Father believes. The salvation of Judah can be found only by worshipping the gods that the people who lived in the land worshipped from its beginning.* But Josiah interrupted his thoughts.

"Those bronze shields that our soldiers carry when they're on parade. I thought Solomon made gold shields. What happened to the gold ones?"

"I'm not sure." Eliakim regained his train of thought. "Didn't Egypt take them?"

"Yes. Pharaoh Shishak attacked Jerusalem and seized all the treasures from the Temple and the palace—and he took the gold shields."

"And Rehoboam made bronze shields in their place. Ah, yes. Now I remember the story." He stopped for a moment, mulling over what he knew about that period. "Why didn't Shishak steal the golden throne?"

"I don't know, but I'm glad he didn't," Josiah answered with a smile as he rose to go. "It's good to talk with you, Eliakim."

"It's good to talk with you too, Father. I wish we could do it more often."

The visit had been a two-way rebuke: the son, that he had been worshipping idols; the father, that he had failed to spend enough time with his son.

"Your Majesty, my scouts have noticed the Egyptian army heading north," the commanding general announced.

"Any sign of their intent?" the king asked. "This is hardly the usual time of year to launch a war."

"Nothing seems apparent. We can observe them only from a distance."

"It's good to keep track of such things. Give my blessing to the scouts and let me know as soon as you get any more information."

Josiah had always been hesitant with regard to Egypt. Many of the Judahite kings had made alliances with the pharaohs. Solomon had even taken an Egyptian wife to ensure the terms of his treaty with the Nile empire. But the custom disturbed Josiah. He himself had made many mistakes, and his daily attendance at the Temple service revealed the cry in his heart to God to forgive him, and to give him strength to be faithful. But God had told His people never to make an alliance with another nation, and Josiah had observed the divine command.

In a quiet moment Josiah thought about the words of Yahweh, uttered through the prophet Huldah, more than a decade before: "I am going to bring disaster on this place and its people. . . . Because they have forsaken me and burned incense to other gods, . . . my anger will be poured out on this place and will not be quenched. . . . Because your heart was responsive and you humbled yourself before God . . . , and because you . . . tore your robes and wept in my presence, I have heard you, declares the Lord. Now I will gather you to your fathers, and you will be buried in peace. Your eyes will not see all the disaster I am going to bring on this place."*

Josiah had often pondered the divine message: "You will gather to your fathers, and you will be buried in peace." *It's such an encouragement,* he thought, *to know that I will be buried in peace, and to know that I won't have to see the nation destroyed.*

Somehow his mind held them as two distinct events with little relation with each other.

The commanding general rose to his feet as the nation's leaders met together in the council chamber. "I have reason to believe that the pharaoh is planning to attack Judah," he began. "My spies have heard rumors that his attendants speak of the pharaoh's desire to add Judah to his kingdom. Egypt has had a long history of meddling in the affairs of our land." He sat down to allow others to speak.

"Perhaps that's why his army advances up the King's Highway," Shaphan suggested. "They haven't as yet reached our borders, but it will be only a few days before they will be upon us."

The prime minister cleared his throat. "I think it's time that we muster our army and prepare to engage them if they seek to invade our territory."

"Sounds like a good idea," the commanding general announced. "We could march our army inland, parallel to theirs, so we'd be ready to meet them if they should attack us."

"It seems reasonable," the king observed. "If we did that, we'd be ready for whatever they decide to do. If they want Judah, they'll pay dearly for it. And by God's grace, we'll prevail."

Josiah returned to his private quarters for a rest. He slept for nearly an hour, but it seemed but a moment before his mother said quietly, "It's time for the evening service."

Zebidah and Hamutal appeared with the children, and, rising, the king joined them, leading the way. The older three boys no longer joined them, as by now they had married and had families of their own.

Jedidah walked beside the king, the place of honor. As the queen mother, she was the most powerful woman in the kingdom, even above Josiah's wives. But she wielded her power quietly, merely making suggestions from time to time. She never worked openly. Instead she acted kindly and gently with all she met.

Josiah appreciated his mother's manner, and often sought her counsel. After the service at the Temple, he asked her to join him in his chamber. "Mother," he began, as they sat down facing each other, "our nation is facing a grave situation, and I need your counsel."

"What is it, my son?"

The monarch related to her the discussions of the council, explaining what it would mean if Egypt attacked the nation. "Many of our men will die, and we might fail. It seems unthinkable that Egypt could have control over our nation—including the possibility that they might force idolatry upon our people. I believe we have enough soldiers to match the enemy, but Egyptian troops seem to be capable of trouncing armies far larger than theirs. Their tactics are different from ours, and even when we try to use their strategies, they don't seem to be as effective for us as when they employ them."

"You believe that Egypt would win if you sought to defend Judah against them?"

"I don't know." He buried his head in his hands. "I just don't know. I would hope not."

"Yahweh has promised that He will protect us from any enemy. Don't you remember how He worked for Jehoshaphat? He destroyed the enemy even before Jehoshaphat's army reached the battlefield."

"Yes"—the king raised his head and looked into his mother's eyes—"I do remember. And I believe that Yahweh will bless us and protect us. But the question I have is this: How can I know what He wants me to do? If I lead God's army into a battle that He has not intended for us to fight, can I expect His protection?"

"Perhaps you should discuss this with Jeremiah or Zephaniah. They may have word from the Lord that will help you decide."

Josiah leaned back. "That's good counsel, Mother. Thank you."

"The Babylonians have destroyed Nineveh," a messenger reported. "The word among the caravans is that the Assyrians have fled north to Haran. The consensus among all our sources is that they don't see how the Assyrians can hold out at Haran because the city doesn't have defenses as strong as Nineveh had, and the Babylonians have a huge army."

"Thank you for the information," the king said after the messenger finished. "Keep in touch with our agents and let me know what happens."

As the messenger left the room, Josiah considered what the man had said. *If the Babylonians have destroyed the Assyrians, they must be a powerful nation,* he thought. *Is it possible that Pharaoh could be moving north to help the Assyrians? to preserve Assyria as a "buffer" between Egypt and Babylon? Could it be possible that Babylon is that much to be feared?*

He paced the room. Suddenly he slammed his fist into his other palm. "That's it!" he thundered. "If Babylon destroys Assyria, it will remove one of the greatest dangers we face. And if that's the case, then we must stop Egypt from linking up with Assyria against Babylon. Should the alliance succeed, Egypt will return to sweep Judah into its fold."

As Zebidah passed the room she saw her husband apparently talking to the opposite wall. "Are you all right, husband?" she asked tentatively.

Surprised out of his reverie, Josiah whirled to see who had spoken. "Oh, it's you, Zebidah." Relaxing and smiling, he approached and kissed her on the cheek. "What does my beloved desire?"

"I merely heard you talking and hadn't noticed anyone enter. I wanted to see to whom you were speaking."

"I guess I was talking to myself."

"What you were saying sounded frightening. It seems that our nation is on the brink of losing its sovereignty."

"You use such complicated words."

"Sorry." She blushed. "I meant freedom."

"I know."

"But I only felt concern . . ."

"Thank you, my love." The king turned from her to pace the room once more, but was careful not to talk out loud. Zebidah passed on down the hall.

The commanding general stood with the king at a large table on which they had spread a rough sketch of Palestine. "The Egyptians have reached Gaza and seem to be in a hurry," the military officer reported. Although he was beginning to show his age, he was still a physically strong man. "It's still not evident what their purpose is."

"I've been thinking about that." Josiah related his thoughts of the preceding day.

"That makes sense. But what if we stop them? They wouldn't be able to link up with the Assyrians, and that cursed nation would . . ."

"Come to its end." Jeremiah joined the group. "But what about Babylon? If Assyria falls, then would Babylon follow up by attacking us?"

"We'd have to cross that ravine when we get to it," returned the general. "But it seems to me we need to stop Egypt from taking over Judah . . . or from linking up with Assyria in order to preserve that nation."

"Have you counseled with Yahweh about this?" Jeremiah smiled. "He can save us from Egypt or Assyria, just as he did in the days of Hezekiah—or even from Babylon. We only need to trust in Him."

"True," Josiah acknowledged. "Would you pray for us, Jeremiah? We want only to do God's will."

But Josiah did not later ask if Jeremiah had received an answer.

---

* 2 Chronicles 34:24-28, NIV.

Chapter 15

A Living, Moving Thing

The commanding general ran his finger along the sketch, tracing the line that represented the King's Highway. "Look at this," he said to Josiah and Jeremiah. "The Egyptians seem to be sticking with the King's Highway at the present. There's no indication that they intend to penetrate the central highlands." He bit his lower lip. "So if they follow the King's Highway, it will lead them to Megiddo . . . and across the valley, and over the Jordan into Syria, where the Assyrians have fled for refuge. We don't usually interfere with armies that use the King's Highway, even though it does lie on our soil. But when they enter our territory from Megiddo to the Jordan, that's another thing. Throughout that area they will have plenty of opportunity to turn south and attack our northern territories."

"And even if they don't," the king added, "and they link up with Assyria, we could face our old enemy again."

"I think we have little choice here." The general unconsciously stood at attention. "I believe we need to meet them at Megiddo. By doing that, we will accomplish two goals: we will protect our homeland, and assure the destruction of Assyria."

"I suggest you move with caution," Jeremiah counseled, "and keep close to Yahweh at every moment."

The king stroked his chin. "Good advice, Jeremiah. Pray for us as we move ahead with our plans—that God's plans will become our plans."

A Living, Moving Thing

How can God's plans become our plans? Will the Almighty stoop to enter our minds and work through us? That seems to be what Jeremiah is implying. Josiah quietly entered his private quarters, deeply immersed in his thoughts. And yet, even then, he had not asked Jeremiah exactly the nature of God's plans. The king already had his mind made up as to what he would do.

Hamutal walked beside him, but he seemed unaware of her presence. "What are you thinking about?" she whispered.

Startled, Josiah looked at her, then smiled. "I guess I did seem rather preoccupied, didn't I?"

"Yes, and I feared to break the spell." He could see a sparkle in her eye. "But it's time for dinner," she continued. "Everyone is waiting for you."

Hastening toward the dining room, the king shot over his shoulder as Hamutal hurried to keep up, "Then let the party begin!"

Everyone heard him and laughed. As he sat down, the room suddenly erupted with the chatter of the children, along with the requests of adults for the servants to bring the food. "Wait," Josiah signaled with uplifted hand. "Let's thank the Lord for His food."

Everyone quieted immediately, and he raised his eyes and his hands toward heaven: "O Yahweh, our Creator God, thank You for this food. Bless us as we eat it. Amen."

And all the family repeated, in chorus: "Amen."

The commanding general summoned his officers from every part of the kingdom. The men, dressed in full battle gear, gathered together in the open plaza just inside the East Gate. They stood at attention, awaiting their orders. Few had any doubts as to the current threat, for the approach of the

Egyptian army could not be kept a secret. It was the anxious topic of many conversations.

"Men, Egypt is at this very moment marching up the King's Highway," the military leader explained. "We do not know their objective, but we cannot exclude the chance that they intend to attack us."

"What can we do?" Shaphan asked. Although he was a priest and scribe, he was also one of the nation's leading generals.

"The king and I feel that we should assemble the army and follow them, paralleling them in the hills as they travel north along the coast." He cleared his throat. "If they do not turn inland before they reach Megiddo, we will surely meet them there, for the King's Highway goes through the Megiddo Pass and into the Jezreel Valley at that point."

"That's more than 50 miles north," another general observed. "That's quite a march."

"Will King Josiah go with us?" someone else asked.

"Of course," the commander answered. "He wants to make sure that Judah is completely safe. And there's another thing we need to consider. Egypt may be moving north to join with Assyria. Our old enemy is losing the war with Babylon in a disastrous way, and has now retreated into Syria. His Majesty believes that Egypt may be going to the aid of Assyria in their struggle with Babylon." The officer studied those in front of him. *Each of these men represents many trained warriors,* he thought, *many of them farmers, merchants, and craftsmen, to be sure, but schooled in battle as well.* "It seems that Egypt wants Assyria to be kind of like a buffer, a strong enough nation that would keep Babylon away from Egypt."

"Why would Egypt be so afraid of Babylon?" Shaphan asked.

"I'm not completely sure." The general stepped back and bowed to Josiah as the king joined him.

Josiah wore his battle dress so as to show that he was one with them. It consisted of a bronze helmet, with leather lining; a bronze breastplate with a thick, hardened leather lining over his tan tunic; and a leather "skirt"—four leather plates hung front and back and along both sides. A leather belt from which hung a sheath that held his sword encircled his waist. The sandals on his feet were fastened with strong leather straps. At 39 he stood tall and strong, his hand resting on his sword.

"Babylon has a powerful army." The king spoke in a soft, level voice, but the men were very quiet, and they could hear him even near the gate. "Like Assyria in the days of Hezekiah, Babylon has a fierce fighting force." Taking a deep breath, he continued. "Babylon may be powerful, but she is ridding the world of the nation that has plagued us for more than a century. And anyone who comes to the aid of Assyria is, for that reason, our enemy."

"Are you saying, Your Majesty," one of the officers from Benjamin asked, "that whether Egypt attacks Judah or plans to join Assyria to fight Babylon, we'll engage them anyway?"

"Yes."

"Then I believe we're in for the fight of our lives."

"You have said it."

Military couriers rushed the news to every city, town, and village in Judah and Benjamin. They also traveled north to Samaria and Galilee, seeking assistance from the newly joined tribes in those areas. Even lonely farmers who tended their herds in the desert received the call to arms.

Men assembled by the thousands, coming from all areas of the kingdom and bringing their battle gear. They carried shields made of a tough, light wooden frame that had thick, hardened leather stretched over it. Light but strong, these shields could fend off spears and swords, and stop arrows—though such missiles could penetrate to about half shaft, and wound the shield bearer.

Some soldiers brought slings and a pouch with a number of stones. The stones ranged up to the size of a person's fist, so slingers could carry only a few. They counted on finding stones at the battle site. It was said that some of these men could sling a stone at a hair . . . and not miss! A good slinger could hurl a stone 70 miles per hour or more.

Each man carried a sword or a knife, with a sheath attached to his belt and tied by a cord to his leg—so it wouldn't flap about during the march. Swords came in all shapes and sizes, depending on the desire of its owner, or its condition when he bought it. Many had short swords—excellent for close, hand-to-hand fighting. Others preferred long swords, a good choice for attacking the enemy while keeping him at a little more distance. Some wielded crude spears as well—shafts of wood sharpened to a needle point, or ox-goads with metal tips.

Each soldier carried a knapsack or basket in which he had tucked a blanket, personal items, and often barley cakes and dried meat or fish—enough to feed him for the start of the campaign. Most of their food they would have to find along the way.

"Father," one the girls asked, "will you be away very long?"

"I hope not." Josiah kissed her on the forehead. "I should be back in a few weeks."

"But that seems so long," one of his older sons objected. "Why will it take so long?"

"We have a long way to march, and then we'll probably have a battle."

"Will you get hurt?" A child began to cry.

"I hope not." The king had tears in his eyes.

After kissing each child on the forehead, he embraced his wives and his mother and kissed each one on the cheek. "Pray for me while I'm gone."

With that, he strode out of the palace.

Within days a large force had gathered north of Jerusalem, ready to march. At the signal of King Josiah, the multitude began to move.

In spite of its size, the army moved swiftly, covering 12-15 miles a day. Couriers and scouts brought news hourly of Pharaoh Necho and his army and their advance up the coast.

"We must hurry so that we can cut Egypt off at the Megiddo Pass," the commanding general urged.

Egyptian scouts followed Josiah's troops as well. Necho knew that he would likely have a serious battle on his hands at Megiddo unless he could avoid it by diplomacy. He sent his personal messenger.

"We have no quarrel with Judah. Nor do we seek any harm to your nation. Please allow us to pass through the Megiddo Valley on our way north. Our objective lies elsewhere."

"I'm sure of that," the king commented to the commander as his scribe read the message. "He's going to Assyria's aid, just as we feared."

Quickly dictating a note to the scribe, he handed it to the Egyptian courier. "I will not allow you to pass through Megiddo Valley," it read. "If you do, you trespass on Judah's soil, and must pay for your crime in blood."

The Judahite army continued north, hurrying to reach the Megiddo Pass before Necho.

Soon another Egyptian courier advanced toward Josiah's

chariot. "You cannot stand against my forces," his message read. "You will surely be defeated, and thousands of your people will die. Turn aside and allow my army to pass."

"Your request is denied," Josiah answered. "You shall not darken our soil with your feet."

Early the following morning, having reached the entrance into the Megiddo Valley, the Judahite forces folded their tents, ate a hastily prepared breakfast, and gathered into ranks. Before they could set out, another courier approached.

"This man seems to have nothing to do but write letters," Josiah muttered.

The courier rode up to the king's scribe and delivered yet another warning. "I had a dream last night," it declared. "A bright being asked me to tell you that your God orders you not to fight me. Only pain and disaster await you at Megiddo if you seek to impede my army."

Josiah remembered again the words of Huldah the prophet: *You shall die in peace; you shall not see the destruction coming upon this nation. Die in peace . . . not in war? What does it mean?* Turning to Eliakim, his son (now 25 years old) who had accompanied him as his attaché, he said, "Necho claims to have had a vision from God that I shouldn't fight him." The king spit on the ground. "How could God speak to a pagan and pass by me and my prophets?"

"It's possible, Father," Eliakim replied. "It would seem that God has the right to choose whomever He wants to be His messenger."

Scowling, Josiah turned to his scribe and dictated: "None of your arguments will deter me. I will not allow you to pass through the Jezreel Valley."

Josiah's army moved swiftly northwest. With room for the army to spread out, the forces advanced more rapidly. Mile by mile they neared the fortress of Megiddo, where Josiah had garrisoned 100 men.

"Should Megiddo's defenders remain in the city?" the commanding general asked Josiah.

"Yes. If some of Necho's forces decide to attack the city, we'll need our men on the ready." After thinking for a moment, he added, "Perhaps we need to send them reinforcements while we can. Have a regiment of 1,000 join them in the city."

"Done, Your Majesty."

Chapter 16

A Deep Mourning

Up the valley moved the Judahite army, a living, moving thing, dangerous to its enemies, the hope of victory to its friends. Megiddo came into sight. No Egyptians. The reinforcements could be seen filing into the city.

The king remained silent for many minutes, thinking. *When we enter into battle, I'll be the focus of Necho's elite forces. I'm sure he'll send commandos with the strict orders to kill me. "Smite the shepherd, and the sheep will scatter."**

Turning to the commanding general, he said: "Necho will seek to kill me early in the battle." He paused to choose his words carefully. "It seems to me that if I'm killed, the army will break ranks . . . and all will be lost."

"We have our most battle-hardened men amassed around you. They can ward off any commandos Necho may send." The officer paused. "At any rate, the men will be encouraged to see their king fighting in the forefront. The king always leads his army."

"Still . . ." Josiah scanned the horizon. "If I were to join the ranks as a regular soldier, it would frustrate Necho's plans and slow his advance. It would force him to regroup, to reconsider what to do."

"That's dangerous, Father." Eliakim had overheard his father's plan. "Remember Ahab? He disguised himself as a soldier instead of leading the troops as their king. Even at that he died from an arrow shot randomly by an enemy archer."

"Yes, my son. But Ahab was a pagan." He thought for

a moment. "Anyway, God promised me that I would die in peace."

"Necho may be right," Eliakim pressed. "If you go against God's command, how can He save you to die in peace?"

"God is with *us*," Josiah chided. "*Not* with Necho."

Without saying another word, Josiah slipped out of his royal robes. He handed them to Shaphan. The scribe's mouth dropped open in surprise. The king now appeared to be just another officer in a chariot.

Just then a cry sprang up from the advance scouts. "Egyptians! They're just coming through the pass." War trumpets began to sound.

Shouts erupted on every side. Officers ordered their troops into prearranged formations, the most experienced warriors stationed in the forefront, for they would be most likely to do the most damage to the enemy. They had trained in the use of arms and in the instinctive movements needed to avoid contact with enemy weapons. A sharp-eyed warrior could even spot an approaching arrow and sidestep it, or at least let it impale only his shield.

Josiah had been in a number of skirmishes, but always as leader—riding in his chariot, beside the commanding general.

The two armies advanced, the gap between them narrowing with each step they took. When the distance between the armies came within about 100 cubits, each side ordered a charge. The command echoed down the line from one officer to another. But the repetition was unnecessary. The order had unleashed the tension that had built up in every soldier as they anticipated the battle.

Bodies hurled forward toward the enemy, clashing midstream, while volleys of Egyptian arrows arched over the front guard, striking down soldiers everywhere. Judahite archers returned the fires, cutting down Egyptians with withering exactness. The slingers went to work on the sidelines, hurling their stones with pinpoint accuracy, aiming directly at the fighting men in the front lines, knocking out scores of the finest warriors of the Nile.

The sound of battle deafened Josiah. The shouts of fighting men; the continuous slap of swords on leather shields; the whistling of passing arrows; the twang of bowstrings, the cries of the victorious, the wounded, and the dying . . . it was almost overwhelming. Josiah urged his chariot forward until he reached the front and entered the fray. Dead and dying lay all around.

Thud!

It hit like the blow of a fist. Josiah took a quick breath . . . his knees buckled . . . his vision dimmed . . . his hand moved instinctively to the arrow that protruded from his abdomen . . . the stinging sensation took his breath away . . . he felt ill . . . he began to vomit . . .

His thoughts wandered. *Hit . . . I've been hit . . . hurt . . . pain . . . need to lie down . . . O Yahweh, help!*

"Bring his other chariot!" Shaphan yelled, dragging the king out of his chariot and back from the front lines. He did not need to speak again. The commanding general had seen, and winced as if he himself had been struck.

The king had fallen!

The arrow had passed through between two of the metal breastplates of his chest armor. The wound was mortal—he had no chance for survival.

As Josiah's second chariot approached, the commanding general helped its skilled driver to maneuver it to within a few cubits of Josiah as the battle waged all around. Willing hands carried him, gently laying him on its floor.

"Take him to Jerusalem—hurry." In his heart of hearts the commanding general knew they now had little chance of winning the battle without their king. Desperately he stepped up into the royal chariot, shouting to the troops, attempting to press the battle forward.

But word spread with lightning speed from one man to another: "The king has fallen! . . . The king has fallen!" And the eyes of the Judahite warriors began to follow the chariot carrying Josiah instead of pressing the battle.

Soldiers broke off from the enemy and began to make their retreat. Soon it became a rout, as more and more Judahites turned to run—in all directions at once. Egyptians followed closely and sought to inflict as many casualties as they could. They would have annihilated Judah's defenders had not Necho called them off. He needed his army. And he needed to continue north.

Both sides fled the battlefield, leaving the dead and dying on the ground. The Egyptians disappeared down the Megiddo Valley.

I've never been in such intense pain, Josiah thought as the chariot bounced over the rough road toward Jerusalem, still 50 miles away. They had already rumbled along for hours, and each bump, each sideward jostle, stabbed him as intensely as the original wound.

O Lord, You've abandoned me . . . You haven't kept Your promise! . . . I've served You all these years . . . destroyed all the pagan altars . . . rid the land of idols . . . brought Your people back to You . . . why have You not kept Your promise? . . . "You will die in peace," You said . . . This is not peace! . . . Or . . . perhaps I shall not die?

"You've been the best king Judah has ever had," Eliakim said as he rode alongside his father, trying to grasp what had happened. "You've served Yahweh all your life. And now, look what God has done to you. What kind of God is that? He's no God at all! He had you destroy all the gods that really mattered, and then He left you to die on the battlefield!"

"Eliakim, don't say that . . . It's not true! . . . It hurts . . . it hur . . ."

"Look at you," the younger man continued. "Dying from a battle wound, suffering because you disobeyed God when Necho warned you that you would fail."

"I-i-it wasn't God who spoke to him."

"It came true, didn't it?"

"Our loss . . . uuuhhh . . . had nothing to do with Necho's dream."

"It had *everything* to do with it!" Eliakim spat out the words. "You call him a pagan when his god predicted the outcome of the battle. You destroyed all the true gods of the land in favor of *your* God. I have heard that one of the pharaohs tried to get Egypt to worship only one god—he called it the *true* god. He failed. And you failed too!"

"Go away, my son. You speak evil. I can't listen now . . ."

"As you say, Father. You shall see me no more . . . forever. And I shall take Judah with me!"

O Yahweh, don't leave me now . . . Forgive me. I know You haven't left me . . . You're always with those who trust . . . in You. . . . Why have I been mortally wounded in war . . . when You promised I'd "die in peace"? . . . Why . . . ?

His thoughts cleared for a moment. *There was more to what You said . . . What was it? . . . Yes . . . "I will gather you to your fathers, and you will be buried in peace. Your eyes will not see all the disaster I am going to bring on this place." . . . I will be buried in peace . . . because . . . I will not see the disaster . . . That's the promise . . . Dying in a battle . . . has nothing to do . . . with the promise . . . The disaster! . . . I won't see it! . . . I am dying in peace! . . . Thank You, Lord! . . . . At last . . . You've given me peace!*

Mile after painful mile the chariot rumbled on. His attendants feared that Josiah wouldn't reach Jerusalem alive, and the thought of that caused them the greatest pain.

"Why didn't we guard him better?" the king's charioteer

agonized. "If he hadn't been hit, we'd have won the battle . . . we *were* winning!"

"Don't chastise yourself, driver." The commanding general had caught up with them. "It's not your fault. It's not anyone's fault. The king did what he thought was best."

"It's not . . . your . . . fault," Josiah moaned. "Don't blame . . . yourselves . . . I . . . I chose my course . . . I bear . . . the blame." Every word took his breath away. Every jolt of the chariot made it harder to breathe.

He motioned to the general, who stooped to listen, for now the king could only whisper. "Tell Jedidah I love her . . . the best . . . mother . . . Tell Zebidah . . . and Hamutal . . . and the children . . . I . . . love them . . . Beware Eliakim . . . He will . . . lead Judah away . . . from God . . . Do not let . . . him take the . . . kingdom . . . Give God . . . the glor . . ."

Then he died—within sight of Jerusalem!

As the chariot bearing the now-dead monarch entered Jerusalem, hordes of people followed behind, already in mourning, for a courier had born the dreadful news ahead. Hundreds had torn their clothing and put ashes on their heads, and wailing filled the houses of Jerusalem from the palace on down.

Servants appeared and gently lay the king on a bier. They carried his body into the palace to prepare it for burial. Custom required burial on the same day of death or, if necessary, the following day.

Removing the arrow proved to be tricky, as the head had lodged against bone. They had to rotate the arrow in order for the point to clear the king's ribs. The rest of the preparation was more straightforward. The servants removed the bloody armor and took off his blood-soaked clothing. They washed his body and clothed the corpse in his royal apparel, including a golden wreath on his head. Finally, they put on his royal sandals.

The Temple Gates

Palace guards bore the bier to the Temple court, followed by his sobbing family. Behind them other guards closed the royal gates. Carrying the bier to the center of the courtyard, the guards placed it on an elevated table. Jedidah; Zebidah and her son Eliakim and his wife and children; Hamutal with her sons Shallum and Mattaniah, with their wives and children; the minor sons and daughters of both women—all filed by the bier and then stood together, about two steps behind it.

Musicians played somber music. A Levite, standing on the northern Temple wall, invited the people to view their deceased king. Young and old filed by the bier on both sides, weeping, crying, wailing. Most had torn their robes, and many wore sackcloth. Almost all had sprinkled dust or ashes on their heads; a few men had shaved off their hair.

As the people filed by the bier, palace servants brought food and drink to the mourning royal family. Some people, who had kept their pagan customs, cut themselves, but since God's law directly forbade this, they were not permitted to enter the Temple court.

A nation mourned its fallen leader—the heart and soul of the kingdom. Josiah's 31-year reign had sought to bring the nation back to God—to help it regain its spiritual roots and relearn the very reason for its existence. The king had struggled to lead the people, once again, to the feet of Yahweh, to kneel before their Creator in worship.

Why would God let His chosen fall in battle—to a random arrow of a pagan foe? Why would God allow His army to turn and run from His enemies? Had He abandoned His people? The deep mourning of the people led them to allow the evil claw of anger to grasp their minds, and to blame God for the disaster that had overtaken them.

"Yahweh is at fault!" they grumbled. "God *caused* our king to fall."

Seeds of idolatry began to germinate within the hearts of those who had worshipped Yahweh just because it had been the popular thing to do. Blame, anger, rebellion began to spread through the crowd. Talk of returning to the gods of the land which presumably had gained victory for Judah's armies in the past, flitted from one person to another. Grief had turned to spiritual rebellion.

When the last person had passed the bier, a light drizzle began to fall, as though nature, too, mourned the fallen monarch. Hand-picked guards hefted the bier and solemnly marched toward the royal tombs to the cadence of tambourines and ram's horns. The citizens of Judah fell into line behind the musicians. Step by slow step the multitude snaked its way along the crooked path that lay along the mountainside.

Reaching the royal tombs, the guards who carried the bier entered the rock-cut, cavelike chamber below the royal gardens in which Josiah's father, Amon, and grandfather, Manasseh, had been buried. Carved into the sides of the tomb were bench shelves where the body would lie. At one end of each shelf the workmen had carved a rounded pillow on which the head of the dead would be laid. A place had also been hollowed out beside the pillow in which an oil lamp was set and lit, to burn continually until it ran out of oil.

Attendants had wrapped the body with bands of linen. As they laid Josiah on the ledge above the dry bones of his father, they placed more than 100 pounds of spices and perfumes on and around the body—to overcome the stench that would permeate the cavern as the body decomposed. Beside Josiah's body the servants placed his personal things: his sword and shield, his seal-ring, his personal jewelry, his sandals, and other items.

Finishing their task, the royal guards placed a stone over its entrance. The crowd dispersed, and only two guards stayed behind, to assure that vandals wouldn't desecrate the tomb.

Jedidah, Zebidah and Hamutal, the children, and the few who had been close to him as friends or government officials lingered near the tomb. The priests and Levites who had been in charge of the daily sacrificial service during the wake now joined them, but remained only a short time.

As the sun set, all but the guards dispersed to their private chambers.

The king is dead . . . long live the king!

---

* See Zechariah 13:7.

Epilogue

Judah virtually died with Josiah. The nation's grief was profound, and Jeremiah poured out his lamentations for his 39-year-old king who had brought religious and political unity to the nation. But Josiah's death also brought an end to his reforms, because Eliakim (later renamed Jehoiakim) led the people back into idolatry.

If Judah had continued to worship Yahweh as Josiah had taught them, it may be that the doom to which God eventually allowed them to succumb might have been avoided. According to the divine law of the conditional nature of prophecy, had the nation repented and refused to abandon God again, the prediction of their destruction might have been overridden.[1]

The people honored Josiah's dying request, though, and Eliakim did not become the next king. His younger brother, Shallum, oldest son of Hamutal, ascended to the throne under the name of Jehoahaz. Although Eliakim must have been disappointed and even angry at being passed over, Scripture offers no evidence of any attempted coup.

Far to the northeast the Babylonians routed Necho and the Assyrians, perhaps as a result of the Egyptian losses in both time and men at Megiddo. One record tells that Necho did not even arrive on the scene until after the battle had already been fought against the Assyrians, with their leader Ashuruballit falling back to Riblah in Syria.

Necho may have been upset by the turn of things, and

that may have had something to do with why he summoned Jehoahaz—who had been on the throne for only three months—to appear before him. He deposed the young king and replaced him with his older brother, Eliakim, whom he renamed Jehoiakim. Necho carried 22-year-old Jehoahaz and his wives and children to Egypt. There they died, never returning to Judah.

Egypt's dreams of reestablishing its ancient empire were short-lived. In 605 B.C. Nebuchadnezzar defeated Necho at Carchemish, and in the following year he advanced southward to the coastal plain of Philistia, seizing the Gaza territory claimed by Egypt.

By pledging himself vassal to Nebuchadnezzar, Jehoiakim spared Judah from attack during this campaign, even though he had to give 10,000 of his best people as hostages—including Daniel and his friends.

But when Necho and Nebuchadnezzar fought to a draw in 601 B.C., Jehoiakim rebelled, and once again declared Egypt as Judah's protector. Not yet ready to tie up his armies in the central hill country, Nebuchadnezzar satisfied himself with ordering his vassals in Ammon, Moab, and Edom to attack Judah.

Jehoiakim reigned for 11 years, until Nebuchadnezzar's general ended the king's rule in 598 B.C.

Jeremiah prophesied in agonizing words that unfaithful Judah would suffer an ignominious end:

> "Announce in Judah and
> proclaim in Jerusalem and say:
> 'Sound the trumpet throughout the land!'
> Cry aloud and say:
> 'Gather together!
> Let us flee to the fortified cities!'
> Raise the signal to go to Zion!
> Flee for safety without delay!

For I am bringing disaster from the north,[2]
even terrible destruction.

"A lion has come out of his lair;
a destroyer of nations has set out.
He has left his place to lay waste your land.
Your towns will lie in ruins without inhabitant.
So put on sackcloth,
lament and wail,
for the fierce anger of the Lord
has not turned away from us.

"'In that day,' declares the Lord,
'the king and the officials will lose heart,
the priests will be horrified,
and the prophets will be appalled.'. . .
Look! He advances like the clouds,
his chariots come like a whirlwind,
his horses are swifter than eagles.
Woe to us! We are ruined!
O Jerusalem, wash the evil from your heart
and be saved.
How long will you harbor wicked thoughts?
A voice is announcing from Dan,
proclaiming disaster from the hills of Ephraim.
'Tell this to the nations,
proclaim it to Jerusalem:
"A besieging army is coming from a distant land,
raising a war cry against the cities of Judah.
They surround her like men guarding a field,
because she has rebelled against me,"'
declares the Lord.

The Temple Gates

> "'Your own conduct and actions
> have brought this upon you.
> This is your punishment.
> How bitter it is!
> How it pierces to the heart!'

> "Oh, my anguish, my anguish!
> I writhe in pain.
> Oh, the agony of my heart!
> My heart pounds within me,
> I cannot keep silent.
> For I have heard the sound of the trumpet;
> I have heard the battle cry.
> Disaster follows disaster;
> the whole land lies in ruins.
> In an instant my tents are destroyed,
> my shelter in a moment.
> How long must I see the battle standard
> and hear the sound of the trumpet?"[3]

---

[1] See Ezekiel 18:5-27.

[2] Babylon lay far to the east, but the army had to march northwest up the Euphrates to Carchemish, and then south (from the north) to reach Judah.

[3] Jeremiah 4:5-21, NIV.

FAMILY BIBLE STORY
SERIES

O ne of the most extensively researched Bible story books on the market today, this series offers features which give background information to engage every member of the family, young and old alike. Written by Ruth Redding Brand and illustrated by distinguished artists, these carefully researched and beautifully illustrated books will make Bible characters come alive for your children. Every name, place, and custom is carefully explained. Hardcover. Available individually or as a set.

Abraham, 109 pages. ISBN 0-8280-1856-1
Adam & Eve, 95 pages. ISBN 0-8280-1850-2
Jacob, 127 pages. ISBN 0-8280-1852-9
Joseph, 87 pages. ISBN 0-8280-1854-5

Quick order online at www.AdventistBookCenter.com
Call 1-800-765-6955
Visit your local Adventist Book Center®
Or ask for it wherever books are sold

REVIEW AND HERALD®
PUBLISHING ASSOCIATION

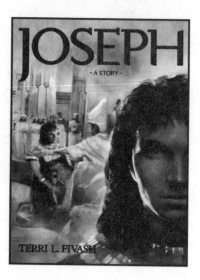

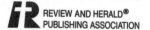

CAPTIVATING STORIES OF GOD'S LEADING

PATTY FROESE NTIHEMUKA

TRUDY J. MORGAN-COLE

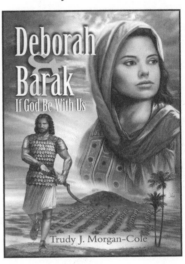

She was a broken, cruel woman. Her heart was numb, and her hope gone—until she met the Man who looked at her with gentle respect in His eyes. This inspiring biblical narrative tells of a woman whose life fully changed after an encounter with the Savior. 978-0-8280-1958-3. Paperback, 160 pages.

She is a prophet. He is a warrior. They have been called to a shared purpose—to help God's people during difficult times. This masterfully written narrative brings to life the biblical account of Deborah and Barak—an amazing story of hope, courage, and God's leading. 0-8280-1841-3. Paperback, 240 pages.

3 WAYS TO SHOP

- Visit your local ABC
- Call 1-800-765-6955
- www.AdventistBookCenter.com

Collect all the Exciting Stories in the Gates Series

SIEGE AT THE GATES
The Story of Sennaacherib, Hezekiah and Isaiah
(released 2007)

THE TEMPLE GATES
Josiah Purges Judah's Idolatry
(released 2008)

FIRE IN THE GATES
The Drama of Jeremiah and the Fall of Judah
(released 2007)

GATE OF THE GODS
God's Quest for Nebuchadnezzar
(released 2008)

THE OPEN GATES
From Babylon's Ashes, Freedom for the Jews
(released 2008)

3 Ways to Shop
- Visit your local Adventist Book Center®
- Call 1-800-765-6955(ABC)
- Order online at AdventistBookCenter.com

Autumn House® Publishing
www.autumnhousepublishing.com
A Division of REVIEW AND HERALD® PUBLISHING
Since 1861